LAURA'S
SECRETS

Augusta Wright

Dream Wolf Publishing

ISBN: 978-0-9982967-0-8

Cover design by Heidi Dorey
Edited by The Authors' Assistant

Printed in the United States

"Do not go where the path may lead,
Go instead where there is no path and
Leave a trail" Ralph Waldo Emerson

CHAPTER 1

Colorado Territory, March, 1867

*L*aura Ralston Brown finished braiding her long blonde hair and pinned it up under her winter bonnet. She studied the red handprint on her cheek in the cracked mirror hanging on the wall near the bed as she wiped the tears streaming down her cheeks. Abner, her husband, was still angry with her this morning for his inability to ride her last night. He had pushed her out of bed onto the cold floor, saying, "Sleep in the rocking chair tonight. You're no good to me."

Obedient to his demand, Laura sat in the rocking chair. Tears streamed down her face as she wept silently, afraid she would bring on more of his wrath. When his loud snoring resumed, she placed logs on the fire, retrieved a quilt from her trunk, and curled up in a shivering ball on the floor near the fireplace. Laura feared she would never see her family again. How her life had changed since her marriage to Abner five years prior. He had been brutal and uncaring for her on their wedding night and the assaults continued. He'd never shown her the least affection. All she ever received from him was verbal and physical abuse of her innocence. Weariness from her daily labors and the warmth of the fire finally relaxed her enough to sleep.

A sharp pain in the small of her back woke her. She cried out and opened her eyes to see her husband looming over her, face purple with rage. "I told you last night to sleep in the chair." He drew his foot back.

Before he could kick her again, she rolled out of the way, but he caught her arm, jerking her to her feet. He slapped her hard across the face. Then threw her to the floor.

"How dare you sleep near the fire," he thundered. "Fry me up some of that slop you call breakfast. We have to get on the road to Everclear by sunup."

She rose, wiping her tear-stained cheeks, and began preparing the breakfast. He always ate more than his share of hot biscuits and crispy fried bacon. She breathed a sigh of relief when he left the cabin to hitch the horses to the wagon for their long trip for supplies.

Laura gazed at the twenty-year-old woman in the mirror, who bore little resemblance to the fifteen-year-old girl forced by her father to marry Abner Brown, a widower with grown children.

~

When they had lived in the city with her family nearby, her husband had limited his abuse to verbal assaults and the occasional quick slap. Then one day, Abner announced they were joining a wagon train leaving Independence, Missouri for California. She tamped down the panic and fear growing inside of her. She did not want to leave her family and go with him, but she had no choice other than to follow where her husband led. And fighting him would only get her into more trouble.

After they left Independence, the trip on the wagon trail was extremely difficult. Neither of them knew how to care for the oxen and the wagon. She walked for miles each day, nudging the team onward. Terrible blisters formed and burst and Laura's soft leather shoes wore out, forcing Abner to purchase boots for her at one of the trading posts they stopped at for supplies. She was expected to cook on a campfire, and there were few times when she didn't burn their food. But they ate it anyway because food and water were rationed as they crossed arid areas without rain. At other times, it rained so much they were forced to wait beside swollen rivers, costing them precious time as the summer drew to a close. Fellow travelers said they'd heard California had pleasant and mild temperatures, but it seemed they would never reach the end of their journey. The more uncomfortable they became and the longer the delays they faced, the more argumentative Abner became. She resisted the urge to fight back because he would hurt her. There was no privacy and she did not want anyone to know he was abusive. So she remained quiet. But, someday she would make him pay. She didn't know how or when, but his time was coming. She turned her thoughts to how beautiful California would be when they got there. The daydreams kept her moving onward.

When their wagon train reached Denver, Colorado, a miner told Abner about a piece of land he had for sale. He enthusiastically described a well-appointed cabin and barn with gold in the streams. He purchased the land sight unseen and unbeknownst to Laura, withdrew them from the wagon train.

When he broke the news to her, she was surprised into challenging his decision. "How could you buy something without seeing it first? And why would he want to sell such a wonderful place?"

He drew his hand back in a threatening manner, but she stood her ground for the first time. "Strike me if you like, but I *will* know why you changed our plans without talking to me first."

To her relief, he dropped his hand to his side, but his glower remained. "I don't have to explain my reasoning to you, but this time I will. The man said he was lonely because he couldn't get a woman to share his home so high in the mountains and under such harsh living conditions."

Laura sucked in a breath, too angry to mind her tongue. "If it was too harsh for other women, why did you think I would like it?"

Abner slapped her hard and she fell backward, hitting her head on the wagon wheel. "Don't ever question my decisions again."

With her head still hurting from the fall, they left the wagon train the next morning, climbing the steep track up the mountains to their new property. To her relief, it did have a sturdy cabin, adequate furnishings, a root cellar, and a well-built barn. Perhaps the miner's tales of gold were true.

Due to their many delays crossing the country, it was already late into the summer, and the miner had done little to prepare for winter. Abner, showing no care for anything but fortune hunting, panned for gold in the river until the heavy snows of a high-altitude winter drove him inside with little to show for his efforts. Laura kept house, using their remaining supplies to make meager meals, all the while wondering what they would do when food ran out.

Their inexperience left them ill-prepared for the long months of isolation and hardships. They had not known to chink the cracks of the log cabin with mortar to keep out the cold or to chop cords of firewood for the times when the snow piled against the door, leaving them trapped for days on end. Being a city girl, Laura had no idea what berries and roots to pick from the forest in the warmer months. Abner did hunt some, bringing in small animals like rabbits, squirrels, and an occasional deer, but it was not enough to last during the terribly long and hard winter. They almost starved to death the first winter. By the grace of God, they survived—stronger and wiser, at least she was.

Three long years later, she'd learned how to plant a garden and preserve everything she grew. Even more critical to their survival, the first spring, she'd encountered Willow, a Ute maiden, gathering healing plants for her mother, the tribal medicine woman. Laura heard her cries as a large bear advanced on her. She shot off the bear's left ear and chased it away from the injured Willow. The Indian maiden's leg was wedged between two rocks; swelling prevented her from moving to escape the bear. Laura used cold spring water to reduce the swelling, lifting the leg up, she wrapped the ankle with strips of cloth from her collection of herbs and salves she had brought with her.

They soon became fast friends. Laura quickly learned all she could from Willow about what could be harvested from the forest as well as the healing properties of plants. Willow also taught her how to set snares for trapping rabbits, birds, and squirrels. Laura's knowledge had been the difference between life and death. Preparation for winter had become the focal point of her existence, with little assistance from Abner who was still sick with gold fever. Willow also provided companionship that enabled her to keep despair at bay in the lonely wilderness.

Laura had not seen her friend since the past fall when Willow was married off to a warrior from another tribe against her will. They'd cried together before they parted. Laura had told her of her forced marriage to Abner, explaining how she continued to try to make the best of a bad situation. She gave Willow the gold locket and chain her mother had given her before she left Independence. Willow had made warm, fur-lined moccasins and woven baskets for Laura as her good-bye gifts. Each promised they would remember the other forever.

Those memories of Willow were precious to Laura as her isolation became overwhelming. She often thought of her friend and prayed her life was going well.

Their closest neighbors were the Wilsons, who lived about an hour away, which, in winter, might as well be the end of the earth. They were as miserable with their way of life as she was. But Mr. Wilson refused to leave the mountains, and his family had no choice but to remain. She prayed they had survived the winter without too many problems.

However, as lonely as she was for human company, she was never without the forest inhabitants she could see and hear all day long. She loved all of God's creatures. She discovered she had special abilities that allowed her to sense their needs and earn their trust. She took pleasure in healing their broken wings or raising the orphaned babies she found. They always drew near whenever she was alone—as if to comfort her in her loneliness.

A large silver wolf had appeared their first spring in Colorado. He lingered at the edge of the forest, watching her. She never felt any fear of him. Why, she did not know, but it gave her peace to know he was near. His name, Silver, came to her as if he had sent it.

⁓

Shaking herself back to reality, she packed the extra bacon and biscuits she had prepared into a basket before Abner returned.

She dreaded traveling in the wagon. The rutted trail was long and hard for this early in the year, and they would be chilled and uncomfortable on the splintery wooden seat. At least the snow was melting early and the days were sunny instead of overcast, but the wind blew cold. Still, their supplies ran low, and they had little choice but to make the trip. Abner always played the part of a caring husband when they were around others, but she knew differently. She was glad to go anywhere right now since she hadn't seen a human face but his since fall.

Ready to go, Laura realized Abner had not brought the wagon up. He'd been far longer than usual. Uneasy, Laura stepped onto the front porch wondering what was detaining him. *Where was he?* Glancing in the direction of the barn, she saw him lying face down in the path.

"Abner, what's wrong?" She grabbed her skirts, running toward his motionless body. She nudged him in the side with the toe of her shoe, prepared to jump back if he grabbed at her. There was no answer or movement. Mind racing, she knelt and rolled him onto his back. Perhaps he'd tripped and hit his head on a stone? She imagined all manner of accidents.

But his glassy sightless stare told her volumes. She trembled in reaction to the flow of emotions—relief, fear, too many to sort out—washed over her. But what had happened? No lump on his head met her probing fingers. Laura looked around the body for animal tracks then checked his limbs for animal bites although surely she would have heard the growls and shouts had he come face-to-face with a bear or other predator. Finding neither, she listened to his chest. Only silence followed. Her breathing quickened as she stood and backed away from his corpse. She was alone, miles from help with no protection. But she was also free of him. He could not hurt her ever again. What kind of a wife had no grief at the death of her husband? She shoved the miniscule feeling of guilt away. A wife whose husband had treated her more like a slave than a helpmeet. Who took every opportunity to demean her or scoff at her attempts to keep them warm and fed through the winters. Who did not deserve her grief.

"Oh my God, thank you!" She raised her arms and turned her face heavenward. "I am free at last." She whirled around, hugging herself. When rationality replaced giddiness, the practicalities took over.

"How can I bury him without any help?" She could always leave him out overnight. The carrion birds and animals would take care of her problem in short order. But she couldn't bring herself to do it—even if it was no better than he deserved. But the ground near their home was solid and still frozen below ground level. Digging a grave would take her many hours and was beyond her physical capacity.

Out of the corner of her eye, she saw the solution.

Last fall, before the ground froze, Abner had started digging a new outhouse hole. With the old privy about to collapse, he had great plans to build a new one. But, as usual, he'd never completed the task. Little had he known, he was digging his own grave. She peered down into the hole; it was deep enough to prevent animals from desecrating his corpse, and the pile of loose dirt next to it would be easy to shovel back in.

The perfect place for a piece of shit.

Laura stood for several minutes, deciding how to proceed. Getting a length of rope from the cabin, she removed his coat and gold watch, dug a small leather bag from his pocket, and then tugged his boots off. The smooth leather under her calloused fingers startled her. When had he purchased new boots? And where had he gotten the money? He'd claimed they didn't even have enough for a little coffee to replenish her dwindling supply. Struggling not to kick the corpse, she tied the rope securely around his armpits. But her dead husband was a large man, far outweighing her, and the soft, spongy ground added to her difficulty. Halfway to the hole, she stopped to catch her breath and considered getting one of the horses to drag him the rest of the way. But, after a few minutes of rest, she continued her chore. Checking his neck and heart again to make sure he was not alive, she pushed him in, feet first.

As his weight came down on his legs, the knees buckled, and his butt settled into the bottom of the pit. When she jerked on the rope, his head drooped over his folded body. Tossing the rope in with him, she shoveled loose dirt on top of his head, hoping the couple of feet between him and the rim of his makeshift grave was adequate to prevent him from being dug up. She'd done her best, considering her ambivalent feelings. Nobody could claim she'd left him for the vultures. What would people think if they knew what she had done? Would anyone care how he had mistreated her? Or about the awful things he had made her do?

When he was covered, she patted the dirt firmly with her shovel, pleased with how she had been able to manage. She outlined the grave with small rocks as if he was lying stretched out in the usual fashion instead of crammed into a shit hole. *Ha!*

Hearing a noise, she looked up to see Silver sitting nearby watching her with his beautiful blue eyes. "Well, what do you think? Did I do a good job?"

Silver only looked steadily at her.

Finished, she picked up his belongings, and with Silver trotting beside her, returned to the cabin. Her winter coat was ragged, and she needed the warmth of Abner's garment. The boots were too large for her to wear, but perhaps she could trade them for a pair her size or other useful items. Pouring a cup of coffee, she sat down in her rocking chair to reflect on what had happened. She was terrified knowing she was alone now, even if she was free. She had never in her young life been on her own and now she was far from any help. What was she to do?

Freedom from Abner created its own set of problems. What protection did she have against a stranger wanting to harm her? Well, if she could shoot a deer to feed herself, she could shoot anyone intending her harm. Still, she needed to be smart about who she let know Abner was dead. How long could she keep it a secret? Would they call her a murderer if she did not tell soon? Why would she? People died in the wilderness all the time.

Seeking comfort, she picked up Abner's Bible from the table near the chair. She'd often wondered how he could read the good book but mistreat her so badly. When she opened it, a letter with her name inscribed in

Abner's spidery handwriting fell into her lap. Odd he'd choose to address it to Laura. All he ever called her was, "Girl."

> *Laura,*
>
> *If you are reading this letter, it means I have died. I decided to write this after I had a bad spell during the winter with lots of pain in my chest. I was not sure if I would recover from it, but I did. I did not want to worry you. I did not know what to do about the situation I had placed us in. I had planned to arrange for you to have the ranch in case something happened to me, but I never did. I ran out of money last year, and my only recourse was to borrow against the land from Tuffy Sawyer at the trading post. A payment will soon be due him, and I have no money. I do not know if any of my grown children would be interested in saving the land for themselves. I don't see any way for you to save it. When you lose the ranch, you can go back to your family in Missouri.*
>
> *Your Husband, Abner Brown*

Laura's emotions ran the scale from hot anger to frozen fear. Glowing hatred began to rise and consume her as she grasped the position Abner had placed her in. The first year here, he had done little to make their life easier. The next spring, he went back to roaming and panning for gold. He found a tiny bit of gold dust in the streams, never enough to meet their needs, but enough to keep him looking. She had begged him to forgo panning for gold and help her with the garden and the tasks she could not do. She'd needed his help to prepare for the winters. However, he would stare at her as if she was stupid and walk off, carrying his shovel and pan to work in the streams all day. She toiled from morning till night to accomplish as many chores as she could. Yet, when he came home, he expected food on the table and her in his bed. And, if she did not have things ready for him, she paid for it.

Laura's deep resentment toward him turned into pure hatred. She felt it growing, becoming overwhelming as she considered all the hurt, abuse, and loneliness she had endured. Jumping out of her chair, she began to pace the room, fighting the desire to go dig him up and...and...What? Cut off his...his...man part? Why? It was useless now anyway. Stab him... shoot him...cut off his head? She didn't know. She wanted to hurt him. She wanted to get even. Then she burst out with laughter at her silly self. *How can you hurt a dead man?*

She continued to pace. "I never thought I would be free of him. I need to control my anger and figure out how I can survive and keep my home." The realization hit her hard. "I have worked too hard on this land to lose it now, even though I am completely alone without family or friends and no money. The possibility of losing her home paralyzed her and she could not move in any direction. *What am I to do?*

The sudden howl of a wolf close to the cabin startled her into action. Hurrying to the door, she opened it and walked out onto the porch. Silver waited nearby for her. She sat down on the step and held her hand out in friendship. She had never touched him before because he always kept distance between them. But now... Silver advanced slowly toward her until he could lick her hand. His adoring blue eyes shone back at her as she stroked his silver fur.

"You wanted to remind me I am not alone, didn't you? Can you read my thoughts? You seem to always be near when I need you. Thank you for being my friend. I certainly need one now."

They sat for some time, together, silently enjoying each other's company. Soon Silver stood up, licked Laura across the cheek in silent farewell, and trotted back into the forest.

Amazed at how a simple act like that could erase her fears and give her encouragement to go forward to meet her future, she went back inside. Picking up the leather bag containing a small amount of gold dust, she was thankful she had thought to remove it from his pocket before she'd buried him. What a misery it would have been to dig him up for this. Taking the bag and his gold watch to the pie safe in the kitchen, she placed them in a small cotton bag and pushed it into the flour bin for safekeeping.

It was too late in the day to go to Everclear. And she was not ready to face Tuffy Sawyer. When she did go, she planned to tell everyone Abner was ill with pneumonia. He was better, but not strong enough for the long trip, so he'd sent her in for supplies. She prayed she could get by with the story. If Tuffy learned he'd died, he'd take the ranch in payment for the debt without giving her a chance to find a solution.

After a good night's sleep, Laura was ready to put her plan into action, and she would need to hitch the team of horses to the wagon to be able to bring back the supplies. Why had she never learned from Abner how to do it? Well, with Willow's help, she'd learned to snare rabbits and hunt and butcher deer—surely this couldn't be harder than that. She walked down to the barn to get the harness and reins for one horse. She would practice on her gentlest mare.

After two hours, Laura and the horse were both frustrated, the patient mare fretful and tossing her head. Wiping tears from her eyes, she put the mare back in the stall and replaced the harness on its pegs and noticed the cradle of the packsaddle.

She would make faster time on horseback, and with her limited resources, she couldn't afford more supplies than a packhorse could carry anyway. She fed both horses and added extra hay. It was once again too late to start out for town, but at least she had a plan.

She went back to the cabin feeling more in control of her situation. The next day, she would take her list and go to the trading post to deal with Tuffy Sawyer.

Leaving before daylight the next morning, she gently nudged Beauty, her mare, down into the river valley, the packhorse following close behind. Loosening the reins to allow the horse to choose the safest path across the bridge in the darkness, she hung on. When they arrived on the other side,

Laura patted the horse's neck, thanking her for taking care of them. Beauty whinnied.

Hours later, she stopped to water the horses in the flowing creek about half a mile from Everclear. She ate a biscuit from the small bag she'd packed before she left. Too nervous to eat more, she washed it down with icy water from the rippling stream. Refreshed, she remounted and straightened her skirt over the long johns she wore for warmth. She checked her pistol, making sure it was primed and ready, then slipped it back into her coat pocket, comforted with the knowledge it was there and loaded. Would she shoot anyone to protect herself? *Hell, yes!*

Arriving in town, she tied the horses to the hitching post and walked up the steps of the massive trading post. Pulling the door open, she was overwhelmed by the disgusting smells flying out at her. The odor of unwashed bodies, vomit from too much rot-gut whiskey, and the stench of fresh fur pelts all contained in a building heated by a large, smoky woodstove.

Laura's first response was to heave, but she recovered and stepped inside. She was sure it had never been aired or cleaned. Several large, hairy trappers dressed in fringed buckskins leaned on the bar with their backs to her, talking and laughing loudly. She slipped into the area of the trading post containing canned goods and other merchandise. Pulling her list from her pocket, she began to pick out the items she needed most.

CHAPTER 2

*L*aura's hand paused in midair as she sensed the evilness invading the trading post. Turning toward the bar, she saw Tuffy Sawyer hiking up his dirty, grease-stained pants. Bales of furs hid her from his view for the moment, but she knew he would spot her before long. A hush descended on the trading post when Laura saw a large, dark-skinned man, dressed in a striped capote reaching to his knee-high moccasins, walk through the outside double doors and to the end of the bar. If she had been nearer to him, he would have towered over her. His faded grey hat with an eagle's feather sewn to the crown was pulled down over long, coarse black hair. His very presence and the intent ebony glare warned everyone to steer clear.

In his right-gloved hand, he carried a long rifle; tucked into the belt at his waist were two long barreled pistols, a large skinning knife, various small bead-decorated leather bags containing lead shot, and a gunpowder horn. Her hackles rose at the dangerous power of this man's presence. The others moved farther down the bar, away from him. He leaned the rifle against the bar and motioned for the whiskey bottle, pouring himself a drink. A match flared when he lit a long, black cigar. The smoke circled his head, creating a mystical halo. Laura stared at the stranger in fascination and a foreboding sense of things to come.

Tuffy Sawyer approached the giant and remarked in a loud voice, "I hope you can pay for that drink, friend."

The silence was deafening. The stranger sniffed the whiskey before setting his glass down on the bar and spoke in a low tone, "I wouldn't have poured it, if I could not pay for it. And I am not your friend."

Tuffy's face turned red. "Didn't mean anything, mister. Have another drink."

The large dark man pushed the whiskey-filled glass toward him. "I want the good stuff, not this watered-down horse pee."

Tuffy replied, "Sure, mister," as he reached under the bar and poured from a different bottle.

When he turned to set the bottle on the mirrored back bar, a hardened voice said, "Leave it! And leave me alone."

"That bottle of bourbon is expensive. Can you pay for it?"

"I told you before, I wouldn't have ordered it if I could not pay."

Tuffy's eyes narrowed when he noticed Laura for the first time. "Well, well, well, if it isn't Mrs. High and Mighty. Where is Mr. Brown, your majesty?" He flashed her a lascivious grin.

"He hasn't been well, so he sent me here to get supplies."

Tuffy approached a man standing near the door and murmured to him. The man turned and left. Tuffy returned to her, grinning.

"What can I do for you today, Mrs. Brown?"

"I have a list." She held it toward him in a shaking hand.

"Well, let's see what you can afford." He walked to the grocery counter, pulled a ledger book from under it, and flipped it open. Running a finger down the page, he said, "It seems, Mrs. Brown, you don't get any more credit until you pay up or you will lose your land."

"Abner found some gold dust, but I don't know how much it's worth." She handed the leather bag to Tuffy.

He poured the small amount of gold dust onto the scale. "Aha," Tuffy declared as he looked at her. "You will have to do better. How about a visit to the back room, and you and me can have us some fun?"

Glaring at him, she pulled Abner's gold watch out of her handbag. "How much will you give me for this?"

Grinning at her, he took the watch. "I'll give you five-dollars credit for it. If you will come to the back with me for the afternoon, it will pay for the rest of your bill and the new supplies, too."

Laura's stomach churned. "Do you treat your trappers and mountain men to an afternoon with you in the back, if they can't pay?"

Several more men had entered the trading post during their exchange. The onlookers guffawed loudly at Laura's comment. Tuffy's face reddened.

"Give me back my watch and gold dust. I'm leaving," she demanded.

"I will not. I'll apply the gold dust and this watch as well as your two horses, which I have had my stable master store in our corral, to your unpaid account," he told her.

Laura stared at him as his words sank in. "What do you mean, my horses? I can't get home without them."

"If you don't pay your account in full by June first, I will take the land and you with it." He turned around, dismissing her.

A blinding rage overcame her. She grabbed one of the cans of beans she had placed on the counter and threw it at his head. He dodged the can as it struck the cabinet behind him. He easily rounded the counter chasing her into the room. She jumped up on the bales of fur trying to stay out of his reach. He grew angry as he grabbed for her, but she continued to stay just out of reach. The trappers were all cheering him on as the show continued.

Tuffy turned to his audience with a snarl. Without thinking of the consequences, Laura leaped on his back, jerking his wool cap off and exposing his ugly, scarred, bald head, which she beat with her fists, scratching him like a wildcat.

He yelled as he fought to sling her to the floor. When he managed to shake her off, she fell onto one of the piles of fur pelts. Seeing his advantage, he leapt on top of her, Laura fought him with all her strength, but it was a losing battle. She clawed at his eyes, making him bellow as a fingernail went into one eye and blood oozed from the cut. She cringed at his rotten breath. He punched her, tore at her clothes, and pulled up her skirt.

Roaring in rage, he jerked hard at her long johns. His face became an evil twisted mask. He slapped her hard again.

Grabbing his knife from his waistband, he said, "I'm going to cut these son-of-bitching long johns off you. If you move, I will cut your throat from ear to ear and watch you bleed out while I fuck you to death. Do you understand me?"

She nodded frozen in terror. The room had become deadly quiet as the trappers were disgusted with Tuffy's intended rape…but no one moved to stop him.

Suddenly, the barrel of a gun was pressed to his temple and the metallic click of the hammer cocking sounded as loud as a cannon. "Drop the knife and get off the lady." said a soft voice.

"Mister you are asking for lots of trouble. Mind your own business and you won't get hurt!" Tuffy remained motionless over Laura.

The gun barrel hit him with a vengeance on his disfigured head, knocking him out cold as he fell forward onto Laura. The dark stranger rolled him off her, allowing Tuffy's large body to tumble to the floor.

Shaking from head to toe, Laura met the gaze of her rescuer. "Thank you so much for helping me. I hope it does not cause you problems, mister." Without waiting for a response, she straightened her clothes, gathered her gold items, and hurried toward the door. Grabbing a wool blanket as she went past a table piled with them, she said to the gaping trappers and Tuffy's henchmen, "Tell Tuffy to put this on my account, will you?"

The stranger let out a loud, hearty laugh as he stood with his hands on his hips over Tuffy's unconscious body.

CHAPTER 3

*L*aura had been unprepared for the disastrous encounter this morning with Tuffy. He managed to steal her horses and hide them. How could she get home without her horses? She'd never make it by nightfall walking. After trudging a distance from the trading post, she wandered for some time in the forest, ending up near the stream as dusk settled in. Gathering enough wood to last through the night, she lit a fire for warmth and to keep wild animals at bay. She sat on a fallen log and wrapped the purloined blanket around her shoulders. Voices startled her from a doze, and she fumbled for her pistol, ducked behind some nearby bushes, and waited to see who had followed her.

"Mrs. Brown, are you here? It's Cora Parker."

Who? She couldn't remember any Parkers, but a woman was unlikely to have pursued her with intent to harm. Laura stood up and lowered her pistol as three women approached. "Who are you? What do you want?"

"As I said, I am Cora Parker, and these are two of my girls, Hannah and Isabel. Hank, who works for me, was at the trading post today and told us what happened. We know Tuffy has taken your horses. Do you have any shelter for the night? I would like to invite you to stay at my house, if you want to. It will be safer than this creek bank and we can see to your injuries."

"I remember you, now. You were in the trading post last fall when we were there. Why would you be kind to me after my husband said those mean things to you?" Laura had been shocked at his ugly behavior toward her, when the woman had only come over to say hello.

"He was afraid I would say something to you about him visiting my girls."

Trying to understand what Cora meant, Laura took her time studying the three women. Cora was older; she wore a white wool shawl across her shoulders, which draped over her beautiful blue silk day dress with a low cut bodice, which revealed enough of her upper torso to let anyone who might be interested know she still had lots to offer. The two younger women were dressed like their employer, but they had a more youthful appearance. Their low-cut silk dresses of red and black, trimmed with white lace along the short hemline, showed their ankles and their wool shawls were pulled tight around their shoulders. Looking at Cora she asked, "He visited your girls for what?"

Cora screamed in delight, "For sex, of course! For his pleasures. Most wives have no idea their devoted husbands would ever think about being unfaithful."

"When? How?"

"The trips he made to town when you were not along. He always came with a pocketful of gold, which he spent on his pleasure. He liked to get rough with my girls, so I finally stopped him from coming back. That was another reason he was rude to me last fall."

"I…I never knew he ever came to town alone. What a fool I've been," she whispered as tears filled her eyes. "I stayed at home and did all the work while he spent the gold he found on his pleasures. I guess he bought his new boots on one of those trips."

"You're not the first wife to be deceived, dearie. Will you come back with us? Are you hungry?"

Laura nodded. "Very hungry."

"Come on then, and let's get back before we freeze to death."

Kicking dirt over the fire to extinguish the flames, she picked up her blanket wrapping it about her shoulders as she fell into step with Cora and her entourage. She had no better options, and got the impression her new benefactor was rarely denied her will.

Gathering her flowing silk skirt, and marching as regal as a queen with her court, Cora led the way to her palace. As they entered through the back door, she began barking orders to any and all around her to cook this and cook that. Before long they were sitting down to a hot meal, with Cora reigning at the head of the table. When they finished the delicious venison stew and hot cornbread, she dabbed her mouth with a napkin and turned her attention to Laura. "Will you tell us about yourself?"

Laura's cheeks heated as all eyes turned to her. *How much should I share?* "I don't have much to tell. I was born in Independence, Missouri. I married Abner about five years ago. He wanted to go to California, but as we traveled on the wagon trail he kept hearing tales of gold in the mountain streams of Colorado. We settled here three years ago. Abner has gold fever real bad. He spends lots of time in the cold streams. This past winter was hard on him, as he took ill with pneumonia. He wasn't …uh… able to come to town today. So I came, and as you know, I am without my horses to get home to care for him." She sniffed, trying hard to fight back her tears.

Cora handed her a lacy handkerchief and asked, "Would you like to work for me until you earn enough money for supplies and horses to get home?"

Laura reacted with surprise, not expecting a job offer, "But what would I do in a house like this? I am not talented like you all. I don't know where to begin."

The women cackled at her statement; they began wiping tears from their eyes.

"I'm so glad I could be the butt of your joke," she said, standing up and knocking over her chair.

Cora leaped to her feet grabbing her in a hug. "We're not laughing at you. We were amused that you said you don't know what to do in a whorehouse. Honey, this is the oldest profession in the world and the easiest to learn. All you have to do is lie on your back while the man does all the work."

"Unless, of course, he wants you to do other things to him with your mouth," added Hanna helpfully.

"Or different positions for you or for him," piped in Isabel.

"What are you all talking about? I don't know anything about these things!" Panic rose at the thought.

"Are you telling us Abner never made love to you?" asked Cora.

"Yes, he rode me. What he did to me never involved love." She set her chair upright, embarrassed at her disclosure, and sank back down before her knees gave way. "Cora, I don't believe I would be able to accept another man in that way, if I have a choice. But thank you for the fine supper and the offer of a job. I believe I'll be returning to my campsite now."

Before Laura could stand up again, Cora replied, "Laura, honey, I have another offer. I need someone to cook, clean, and wash linens around here. I fired my Chinese cook because we were sick of eating nothing but rice. I wouldn't need you to work on your back. I want you to work with your hands."

"Oh, I'm a good cook. I know how to launder sheets and clean a house. Will I be able to earn wages to pay the devil at the trading post?" Laura asked.

"I can pay you with room and board, but, unless our business picks up, I am limited on wages since the gold rush has petered out around here. You could take in laundry from the miners to earn extra money. You will be safe here, and no one will bother you. The room off the kitchen has a lock on the door. All clients go upstairs with the girls. They come and go at all hours of the night, though, so I hope you can sleep soundly." She grinned. "It does get noisy around here on Saturday nights."

"Thank you so much for helping me. I promise you will not regret it." Laura wiped a tear from her cheek when all the girls jumped up from the table, coming around to hug her.

Holding her hand, Cora led her to a beautiful room with frilly curtains and lacy pillows piled high on the blue satin bedspread covering a magnificent, four-poster oak bed.

"Cora, this room is too fancy for me."

"No, it's not. We all have nice rooms. Did you bring any extra clothes?"

Laura shook her head.

"Well, don't worry. We have plenty around here, and some should fit you fine. Now I will be back soon with nightclothes. You must be exhausted from such a long and frightening day. There is fresh water in the pitcher to wash up with while I'm gone."

True to her word, Cora returned with a soft, white lacy nightgown, robe, and warm cozy house shoes. "If you need anything, let one of us know. I'll show you around tomorrow. Sweet dreams!" She closed the door and was gone before Laura could say a word.

Holding the gown and robe, she moved around the room, staring at paintings of nude women and half-dressed men in suggestive positions. Her head turned this way and that, as she wondered how it was possible to accomplish the acrobatics. Her knowledge of what happened between a man and a woman greatly expanded after seeing them. *What a day I've had. I left home this morning to get supplies and now I'm working in a whorehouse. What next?* She removed her clothes, washed up, and put on the lacy nightgown, enjoying the pleasant feel of it. Climbing up the high steps onto the bed, she pulled the covers back, fluffed the pillows, and fell asleep as soon as she stretched out her weary body.

CHAPTER 4

*L*aura hummed as she washed the linens and hung them on the line to dry. She had been at Cora's for a week and had cleaned the house from top to bottom, cooked meals for Cora and the girls, and had taken on the washing. Her thoughts wondered to the mysterious dark stranger. *Who was he? Why did he help me?* Hank told them later the stranger took a squaw chained in the back room of the trading post with him and a load of supplies, but he'd left a five-dollar gold piece. Tuffy Sawyer had gone crazy when he woke up after he was cold cocked. He vowed he would get the stranger and make Mrs. Brown sorry she'd rejected him, too.

Tuffy did not like being the butt of a joke, and especially resented having a woman get the best of him. He would harm her, if he got the chance.

A sound behind her woke her out of her fretting and caused her to whirl around, grabbing for her pistol strapped to her hip.

"Don't shoot! Sorry we frightened you, ma'am. We wanted to ask you if you would help us."

Laura stared, opened-mouthed, at two of the most beautiful men she had ever seen. Even though their hair was long and their faces had several days' growth of whiskers, she saw their warm eyes and pleasant smiles. She felt butterflies in her stomach, and wondered why. Shaking herself she asked, "What do you want?"

"My partner and I noticed you washing clothes and wanted to know if we could pay you to wash ours?"

"Pay me? How much?"

"We've been traveling for some time, and our clothes are pretty dirty. We would pay you fifty cents."

"Each of you would pay me fifty cents?"

"Yes, ma'am. Do you work here?"

"I am the cook and housekeeper. Nothing else."

"Oh! Do you serve meals here, too?"

"No, you can find food over at the hotel restaurant."

"When do you want our clothes?"

"You can leave them now and pick them up tomorrow afternoon." Laura noticed the other handsome man staring at her.

"We will leave the dirty clothes later today, after we buy new ones," said the first man.

"Who are you? What brings you to Everclear?"

Both men whipped their hats off. "I'm Jim McKenna," said the first.

"And I am Rowdy Adams." The muscular sandy-haired man spoke for the first time. "And what is the name of the most beautiful woman in the world?" He flashed her a grin, eyes sparkling.

"My name is Laura Brown." She grew nervous from their nearness.

Both men replied at the same time. "Glad to meet you, ma'am."

"Has there been any gold found around here?" inquired Rowdy.

Laura stiffened. "None I know of. When you return, leave your dirty clothes on the back steps. I will have them ready for you tomorrow afternoon." She turned her back on them, replaced her gun in her waistband, and continued with the washing.

Later that day, Laura watched from upstairs as the men returned. With their faces shaved and hair trimmed, they were even more attractive to her. But she was staying away from men. Even the ones who looked as good as these two did. How educated she was becoming from Cora's girls.

Laura washed the two men's garments, mended anything needing a button or a stitch, and darned the holes in their socks. When they returned the next day, they paid her the dollar and thanked her for her help.

Rowdy said, "Would you honor us by eating supper with us tonight at the hotel?"

"Sir, I am a married woman and not interested in you or your friend. Take your clothes and leave," she retorted.

"Sorry, we didn't mean to offend you. You're so beautiful; we'd hoped you were unwed."

Jim tipped his hat. "Good day to you, ma'am." He pulled a protesting Rowdy in the direction of Main Street.

Laura held her smile in until they were out of sight. *They think I am beautiful. That's one for the books.* She brushed back damp wisps of hair from her flushed cheeks and went back to scrubbing sheets on the washboard. Later she would send Hank with the dollar to give to Tuffy to apply to her account. It was a start.

CHAPTER 5

*L*aura waited patiently for the moment when she could steal back her horses and return home. The horse wrangler always shut the stable doors at dusk to go home for his supper, never returning until the sun came up the next morning. When the time was right, she made her move.

Laura rode like the wind after stealing her horses and tack back the night before. Cora had given her extra supplies and she left before dawn. As soon as the horses were missed, Tuffy sent men searching for her. She stopped often to glance behind her. Sure enough, she discovered two men following her. After a moment of panic, she said a silent prayer of thanksgiving because Willow had taught her how to handle the situation. She sought a large fallen branch. Tying it to the packhorse, Laura dragged it behind her for some time, moving in a haphazard manner through the pines to cover her passage before discarding the limb.

When she reached the path to the cabin, she turned off and dismounted. Tying her horses to a tree away from the main road, she dragged leafy branches across the horses' tracks and scattered handfuls of leaves as a finishing touch. On the off chance the men did not know exactly where her cabin was, she wanted to make sure they did not stumble upon her path by accident. Satisfied, she remounted and rode quickly, hoping to move out of earshot before her horses neighed back at the others.

She tied them to the porch post, grabbed her rifle from her saddle scabbard, and raced back up to the ridge. As she lay on her belly under low bushes, a pair of tough looking men rode passed, leaning low out of their saddles looking for signs of her passage. To her immense relief, they soon disappeared around a bend without looking back.

She stayed hidden for some time, wanting to make sure the men had not detected her home. After a while, she heard hoof beats returning. The men were cussing and talking about what they would do to her when they caught her.

"Think she knows how to shoot, Bart?" asked an evil looking man with a jagged scar over his left eye.

Bart answered. "Probably not, Lefty, but she sure would be good in bed!"

"You wouldn't be very good in bed if'n she shoots off your dick because you misjudged her shootin' abilities," laughed Lefty. She remained in place while they rode out of sight in the direction of town before racing through the brush back to the cabin.

Laura began settling back into her home. She unloaded the supplies Cora had given her, fed her horses, and checked to see how many chickens she had left since she was not here to pen them at night. She was sad to discover two were missing, but the others clucked at her to feed them. The cow had had her calf while she was gone so all was well there. Returning to the cabin, she fixed herself a light supper and settled her nerves with one of her delicious teas. At bedtime, she knelt in prayer thanking the Lord for keeping her safe from harm. She asked Him to help her forgive the hatred she felt for Abner but knew that would be difficult. She gave thanks for her newfound friends at Cora's. Not wanting anyone to know Abner had left her alone and penniless, she prayed for help to keep the ranch. She climbed into bed and was asleep as soon as her head touched the pillow, relieved to be home.

The next morning Laura worked in her garden, preparing it for planting. The day was warm and beautiful as she sowed some of her precious vegetable seeds, saving different types for later planting. She worked hard knowing the growing season in the mountains was short and she wanted a head start.

She heard the cow bellowing and knew she could not put off milking her any longer. What was it about bovines? She'd had many problems with the oxen on the wagon train. She could relate to other animals, tame or wild, but these creatures were a mystery. Picking up the pail, Laura headed toward the sounds dreading each step.

Betsy's calf, born in the meadow before Laura returned, was several weeks old now. She did not like Laura around the newborn and had made a fuss when tied outside the stall and the calf separated from her. She had allowed Abner to handle her without any problems. But anytime Laura tried to milk her, Betsy took every opportunity to step in the half-full pail. If she could kick it over, she would. Now it was solely up to Laura to milk the cow if she wanted any milk and butter. She was as determined as her nemesis—it was going to be her way or else.

When she entered the open doors, she went to get the rope to tie Betsy's hind legs together. She did not want to be kicked or stomped in a stall, so she tied her outside the stall in the open area. If there was trouble, Laura had plenty of room to get out of the way. As she leaned down to tie the hind legs at the knees, Betsy lifted both back legs at the same time catching Laura in the chest, lifting her high into the air, and sending her flying out the open doors.

Landing spread-eagled on her back, she knocked the air out of her lungs and slammed her head hard on the ground.

People said when they hit their heads, they saw stars. Well, Laura could tell those people what she saw were not stars, but handsome male angels and horses' heads hovering above her. *Shouldn't angels have wings? Did angels ride horses?*

There was something so familiar about the two angels. *What was it?* She gave them a silly look as she passed out in their arms.

CHAPTER 6

*L*aura smelled bacon. Did God serve bacon in Heaven? Was she dead? She was so confused. She moaned as she tried to see. Everything was spinning. The motion made her sick to her stomach. Her head hurt and she could not think clearly. How was she to get help? She had no one to send—she was alone.

A cold wet cloth placed on her aching head caused her to moan with relief. The angels were still here.

"What can I do to help your headache? What herb or tea can I fix for you?" She recognized the familiar voice. Opening one eye, she stared at the handsome face.

"Are you an angel?" she whispered.

"Don't you remember me? We met in Everclear when you did my laundry. Tell me what I can fix to make you feel better," the voice was low and close to her ear.

"Oh, I remember you now," she sighed. "Please find the can of willow bark. A pinch in a cup of hot water." Sometime later, she was lifted up and very bitter tea was poured into her throat. She managed to drink half the cup before passing out again.

Much later, Laura woke again. Her head still throbbed, but not as badly as before. A silly memory about angels tickled her mind, but surely she had been dreaming. Someone had spoken to her, brought her tea…. But who?

She heard the cabin door creak and the thud of boots on the wooden floor. Still dazed, she lay still. Who was in the cabin? If she pretended sleep, she could buy enough time to plan out what to do. Someone touched her head, and she jerked.

"Laura, are you awake?" Whoever it was spoke with a southern drawl.

A second, deeper voice said, "I think we're scaring her. We won't hurt you, Laura. As we rode up to your place, your cow kicked you and sent you flying. You landed on your back almost under our horses' feet. Do you remember anything about the accident? That was four days ago."

"Four days ago!" Laura sat up in bed, regretting the movement as she grabbed her head, moaning. Four large, work-roughened hands gently laid her back against the pillows, placing a cool wet cloth on her head as another strong wave of nausea swept over her.

"Will you drink more of the willow bark tea?" the deeper voice asked.

Nodding she whispered, "With honey, please."

After she drank the sweetened tea, the room stopped spinning and she opened her eyes to look at her caregivers. "I remember doing your laundry. But I have forgotten your names."

The large, muscular blond-haired man with the southern drawl looked kindly down at her and replied, "Yes, you did our laundry. Thank you for mending our clothes. I had some missing buttons. I am Rowdy Adams of South Carolina. At present, I am an unemployed soldier looking for work. And this is my friend, Jim McKenna. He was my captain in the Confederacy, hailing from Virginia." He continued softly. "When the war ended, we went to Texas for a spell. We then decided we wanted to see what was out West and to try our luck prospecting for gold."

"Do you remember anything about your accident?" Jim asked her.

Laura rubbed the side of her head trying to think about what had happened. "No, I remember nothing about the accident. How did you find my ranch?"

"Now that is a curious thing," Jim answered. "We don't rightly know. We followed two men Tuffy sent after you. When they didn't find your trail or cabin, we hid out until they gave up. It was almost dark, so we camped near the main trail until morning. The next day, we were heading down the mountain when a large silver timber wolf came toward us. He watched us and ran back into the trees. Then he came back out as if we were to follow him. It was the strangest thing. We're not sure where here is, since he brought us through the forest."

Oh no! "Did you hurt him?" Laura asked in alarm.

"No, ma'am. After he led us to the cabin, he disappeared. Strangest thing we ever saw," said Rowdy. "As we approached the barn, you came flying out."

"Do you feel strong enough to eat? We fixed beans and cornbread."

Laura grinned sheepishly, "I keep smelling bacon. Is there any left?" The two large men dashed around trying to fix her something to eat and drink. They kept running into each other, going from here to there. She lay back on the pillow, amused at their antics, and waited until they brought her a tin plate filled with burned bacon, somewhat watery beans, and overdone cornbread. She ate every bite, starved after her long rest. Strangely, her eyes were already heavy again.

"I need to thank you both for coming to my rescue and for taking care of me. My husband, Abner, had left to go hunting for several days." She stifled a yawn.

"Glad we could help," Jim said. And she drifted off again into a dreamless sleep.

When the clock on the mantel struck five, Laura woke and saw two forms wrapped in bedrolls lying before the fire. At first she was surprised they had slept in the cabin, but they had been taking care of her—where else were they to sleep? She was feeling much better today and would straighten out the sleeping arrangements.

When she tried to ease from the bed, she gasped at a sharp pain in her chest. She probably had cracked ribs as well as other injuries. Slipping behind the privacy screen to dress, she realized she was wearing a nightgown! She had not been dressed for bed when she left the cabin four days ago. How could she face them, knowing they had undressed her? Not even Abner had seen her in the altogether. These men removed her dress and long johns and dressed her in a nightgown. What an embarrassing situation!

She considered several ideas before deciding the best way was to ignore it. They would be on their way soon, and all would be forgotten. As she unbuttoned the front of her gown, she discovered an ugly hoof-shaped bruise above each of her breasts. Betsy had kicked her hard. Thankfully, it had not been her head or she would be dead now. And, she was also thankful to the Lord for sending help. She would think pleasant thoughts about the angel men and Silver for guiding them here.

She had the coffee boiling when they began to stir. They were pleased to see she was up and moving around. In fact, the heavenly smell of biscuits baking filled the cabin. They hurried to help her, insisting she not overdo it. With their help, she soon had a breakfast of bacon, eggs, and hot biscuits with fresh churned butter.

"Thank you for doing the milking and other chores. I was able to make a delicious breakfast this morning with the butter you churned and eggs you gathered."

"It was our pleasure, Laura. Are the biscuits ready yet?"

When they sat down at the table, Laura extended her hand to each man and asked if one of them would offer a blessing for her continued recovery and for the food. Their eyes widened, but Jim spoke a few words of gratitude and they all said amen.

"Thank you, Jim, I appreciate it. I thank you both for helping me. If you hadn't come along, I would have laid there until I could get back to the cabin or was eaten by a wild animal." Jim and Rowdy exchanged glances but remained silent.

After she refilled their coffee cups, Jim asked, "So where is your husband? We know he has not gone hunting. His guns are still on the rack. Aren't you concerned he has not returned?" He searched her face. "Laura, is that a fresh grave behind the cabin?"

Laura swallowed hard before replying. "He died suddenly almost four weeks ago. I did not know he was ill. Or why he died. I didn't want anyone to know I was alone here. I thought if anyone knew they would try to take my ranch. I couldn't understand how you found me until you told me about the wolf."

"You know about the wolf?" Jim asked with disbelief.

"Yes, after we moved in, he began to appear on the edge of the forest to watch me. I feel he has come to be my protector."

They looked at her unable to accept her explanation.

"Wolves, and what other protectors are around here?" Rowdy asked.

Thinking of her forest friends sent a warm glow through her. "Oh, there have been lots of lost or injured animals and birds I've cared for, but Silver is the one I have a strong connection to. He will come to me when I am afraid or lonely and let me touch him. Then he licks my cheek before he goes back into the forest. But even when he's gone, I sense his presence."

She was amused at the expressions on the men's faces of total disbelief. "Don't you believe me?"

"Of course, we saw him ourselves, but we find it hard to believe that a wild wolf has become your companion."

"Well, believe it or not, it happened. How soon will you be moving on?" Laura inquired wanting to change the subject.

"Well, we wanted to talk to you about that." Jim exchanged glances with Rowdy. "We would like jobs here helping you with chores you cannot do by yourself. We need a safe place to stay for a while because the law is looking for us."

These men could be killers sitting here with her. A cold chill ran up her spine. She'd revealed she was alone and unprotected.

They started to talk at the same time in a mixed bag of male voices each trying to outdo the other. It grew louder and louder until...

"Stop, please!" Laura yelled. "One at a time," she said in a quieter tone.

Jim began, "We rode into Denver and stopped at one of the saloons for a drink. Right after we walked in, a man we hadn't seen since the war recognized us and began calling us deserters. He knew it wasn't true, but it was his way of causing trouble. He had been under my command and was a drunkard and troublemaker. His problems were someone else's fault. He grew angrier and pulled a gun on us. We both shot him." He lowered his head, ashamed of his actions.

"We don't like killing. We had enough of it in the war. And we had to do it again. His friends told the marshal we started the trouble and pulled on him first, so we lit out for the mountains. We will give you an honest day's work, and please don't be frightened of us. We would never harm you," added Rowdy in his deep, southern drawl.

Laura did not know how to say what she wanted to say. The silence dragged out and finally the men stood up.

"We'll go saddle up and be gone soon," stated Jim.

"Please sit back down. We aren't through talking. I have a problem, and I've been trying to decide how to say it. However, it seems you have a problem, too. We need to come to an understanding of what each of us needs out of this deal." Laura took a deep breath. "I discovered after the death of my husband that he had mortgaged the ranch to Tuffy. We had been buying our supplies, and whatever else we needed on borrowed money and my husband didn't pay it back with any of the gold he found. Now the payment comes due on the first of June, and I have nothing of value except the horses and the ranch. I need help with chores I cannot do, and, in exchange, I can offer you three meals a day and let you bed down in the barn." If they didn't accept her offer, she'd never be able to keep up the ranch, but she couldn't sacrifice her reputation either.

"The barn!" they chorused.

"Yes, the barn," Laura crossed her arms and looked her sternest. "I will not be sleeping with two strange men in my house. What will the neighbors say?"

"What neighbors?" Rowdy hooted.

"I do have neighbors who drop by to check on us when they can. Although they have not come by in a while, it is about time for them to show up. I don't want them to see me here alone with two men.

"Also, as I told you, no one but the two of you knows that Abner died, and I want to keep it that way for the time being. If anyone comes to visit, please fade into the woods until they are gone. Do you understand?" she asked.

They both nodded.

"Are you still going to make us sleep in the barn?" asked Rowdy with a big grin.

Laura thought for a moment then said, "I will compromise. There is a lean-to on the back of the cabin. It was built for the livestock in the winter when the snows became too high to get down to the barn. There is also a fireplace with the chimney connected to mine. It will be very comfortable once we clean it out. I have quilts to help make a bed of hay more comfortable. How does that sound?"

"Like heaven." Jim winked at her.

What did the gesture mean? Whatever it meant, it made her feel special. No one had ever made her feel special before.

With a happy heart, she gathered the quilts to help them settle into the lean-to. Maybe they *were* angels.

CHAPTER 7

First thing after breakfast, Jim and Rowdy began repairing the barn and corral because no maintenance had been performed on either since Abner and Laura moved in. The barn leaked badly in places and the corral timbers were rotten and needed to be replaced. Laura felt strong enough to work a little in the garden. As the day grew warmer, she decided to take the men some fresh spring water.

The shock of seeing two sweaty, muscular male bodies rippling as they glistened in the sunlight and clad only in pants and knee-high boots almost made her drop the bucket of water. When they turned to greet Laura, she discovered she was eye-level with their beautiful muscular hairy chests. And with each breath, their tawny muscles moved under suntanned skin. The vision reminded her of the paintings at Cora's. Cheeks flaming, she couldn't look away.

Jim took the dipper and said, "Thanks. We were getting hot and thirsty." He took a sip then poured the rest over his head. She watched as the water slid through his black hair, down his tanned face, glided over his neck muscles, and entered the forest of black curly hair on his muscular chest. The little streams of cold water encircled his rigid nipples and flowed down his flat abdomen to the waistband of his pants. The bulge at the juncture of his legs grew larger as Laura continued to stare hotly at it.

Rowdy, wanting Laura's attention, grabbed the dipper from Jim and poured water over his head as well. Laura watched the same sexual glide of the spring water down Rowdy's muscular body and she grew warmer not from the sunshine, but with improper thoughts of where the water was going. When it soaked into his trouser band, it highlighted his enlarged maleness.

Her body betrayed her as she watched the half-nude men; she breathed deeply smelling their male scent. She felt a desire to touch each one and fought the urge to do so. She had been married long enough to know what the meaning of the bulges in their pants meant. Frightened at her own responses and thoughts, she dropped the bucket, as she fled toward the cabin, yelling over her shoulder, "I have to check on the beans before they burn!"

Shutting the door, she held her palms to her heated cheeks. "Oh my goodness, they're beautiful! My angels are like gods. My curiosity will get me into trouble if I'm not careful when I'm around them." She put a pot of beans on to cook so they would not know she lied to get away from them.

They arrived for the noon meal with their shirts on, relaxed and ready to tell Laura about some of their adventures or misadventures growing up in the South. She giggled happily at their tales. They asked her about her family in Missouri.

Laura blinked back unshed tears. "I miss them so much. It hurts to think of them. I am so lonesome for my sister, Jane, who was my best friend growing up. She's the smart one. She has glorious plans for her life." Tears spilled over as she thought of what her life might have been if she had been able to remain with her family. As the tears trailed down her cheeks, she brushed them away saying, "I do get occasional letters from my mother who keeps me up on the family news. I try to write, but we don't go to town often. So when I go, I post all my letters at one time. That way they can keep up with what I am doing here."

Rowdy asked her, "Why did you come West?"

Laura hesitated for a moment. "I didn't have a choice about marrying or coming here. Abner offered to marry me to provide the family with a salary until my father could recover from an injury at work. About three years ago, he announced we were moving West. We've been here ever since."

Laura poured more coffee then cleared the table. When they had rested, Jim and Rowdy went back to work. Thankfully, they said nothing about the water business because she was not sure what had really happened. Wiping the event from her mind, she began to plan the evening meal.

After Laura finished the dishes, she rested most of the afternoon. Later she walked down to the barn to gather the eggs and pen the chickens for the night. Hurrying back to the cabin, she put the final touches on the evening meal. She rang the dinner bell then finished setting the table.

When they entered the cabin, she was placing a huge bowl of milk gravy next to a large plate of elk steak, fried potatoes, and beans. They sat down at the table. Laura joined them and she extended her hands to each man. "Rowdy, will you say the blessing this time?"

Rowdy bowed his head.

The supplies Cora had sent with her and the supplies the men brought were proving to be a big help now that she had extra mouths to feed. She enjoyed cooking a large breakfast and an even larger supper knowing the hardworking men needed more food. One day a week she baked bread. She had to limit the men to one loaf of hot bread as soon as she removed it from the oven or they would try to eat as much as they could. The smell of baking bread whetted everyone's appetite.

Two weeks later, the barn roof and fences were complete. Laura had asked them to enlarge a small existing corral on the front of the barn. Now it was possible for her to see the animals from the cabin without having to go down to check on them. At the upper back ridge of the hidden valley, they built a gate extending it to each side of the steep ridge to prevent the horses from wandering off.

When all the work was completed, Laura felt wonderful. Excited by the new repairs, she grabbed Jim around the middle, hugging him.

Jim had been smiling until Laura hugged him. He gave her the strangest expression. Setting her back from him, he walked toward the river without a word. Rowdy emerged from the storeroom. "Where is Jim going? I thought he was hungry."

"I don't know where he's going." She turned toward the cabin because she could feel her cheeks flaming red. Uncertain what she had done to cause Jim's strange reaction, she wanted to put it behind her until she could find out.

During supper, there was little conversation. After they finished eating, Laura asked, "When will you be able to go hunting? The meat supply is beginning to run low."

They agreed to go after breakfast in two days because they wanted to finish what they had been working on before setting out.

After the evening meals, they usually played poker, trying to teach Laura to keep a straight face if she had a winning hand. But tonight, neither seemed interested in staying in the cabin, not even long enough to help with the dishes like they usually did. She could not put her finger on what she had done wrong by hugging Jim, but she felt she had offended him. She planned to find out the next time she was alone with him, and apologize. She wanted both men to be as happy as she was.

When she finished, she took her cup of coffee out to the porch to sit a spell before retiring. She loved watching the sun sink behind the mountains, casting its final brilliant rays on her world. Her hidden valley glowed warm and alive back at her. From the highest point of the ranch, she could see the trail across the valley edge and know if anyone was coming. The valley had a way of echoing the sound back to her, making her aware of horses and riders. She sat in her rocking chair, enjoying the bliss, when a sound nearby startled her.

Jim came around the corner of the cabin from the lean-to. When she lifted a hand to wave, he turned to go.

Where was he going? Had he come to talk with me and changed his mind?

"Please don't leave," Laura called. "Will you join me? I need to talk with you."

Jim walked up to the porch and sat on the top step, stretching his long legs out in front of him as he leaned back on the post.

When he did not ask her what she wanted, she became annoyed. In frustration, she asked, "What did I do to upset you? Please tell me so I can make it right."

"Being a widowed woman, you don't know? Is this an act? Are you trying to fool us with your innocence?" he barked.

What have I done? "Please, tell me how I am fooling you."

"Are you so dumb you don't know what your touch can do to a man?" he blurted out.

She stood up, gazing down at him, "If I knew why you were acting like this, I wouldn't have asked you what was wrong. You continue to accuse me of something, but I have no idea what you're talking about. So, if you want to play games, then play by yourself because I'm going to bed." She spun toward the door but Jim jumped up, grabbing her before she got halfway there.

He pulled her roughly to his hard body and nuzzled her hair. "When a woman allows a man to hold her like this, it makes it hard for him to control himself. Don't you know? Didn't your husband ever hold you and love you like this?" he whispered between ragged breaths as he rubbed his body against hers. She melted into him.

"There were two times he swung me around when he was happy," she murmured. "Is that what you mean?"

He held her face tenderly in his hands, as he gazed into her eyes. "Are you still a virgin?" She tried to push away from him but he was ready for her reaction and did not let her go. "Laura, I am not asking you to make you scared of me. I am asking because you may not know the effect you have on a man. You are young and beautiful with your sky-blue eyes, honey-colored hair, and a body a man could lose himself in. Don't you understand I desire you?" He lowered his head to kiss her.

His lips were soft and pleasant on hers. She swore she heard harp music all around her. She smelled his clean scent of leather and wood. The demanding kiss and his body pushing into her heating body overwhelmed her senses. She felt wetness between her legs and a yearning that needed immediate relief. She floated on air. The sensations were unlike anything she had ever felt before.

Frightened by these new unfamiliar feelings racing wildly through her head and body, she pushed him away. "I don't need you or any man to turn my head with your sweet words. Now get off my porch!" She stormed into the cabin, shut the door with a loud thud, and barred it.

CHAPTER 8

When the men came to breakfast the next morning, Laura greeted them happily. "Sit down and eat."

They prayed as usual. This time, before releasing her hand, Rowdy looked at it. "How do you keep them so soft and smooth? I know you work just as hard as we do, but ours are so calloused and rough."

She pulled away. "A woman I met on the wagon train was a healer who taught me about herbs and remedies and how to take care of dry skin. If you would like some of the mixture, I'll be happy to give you a small jar of the salve. It would work well for you to apply it before you put your leather gloves on so it can soak into the leather, making it soft, too. Your hands won't crack and bleed anymore."

Rowdy agreed to try it, and Laura got up to get him the salve. Jim remained silent. During the rest of the meal, she asked them questions about the day's activities.

After Jim headed out the door in the direction of the barn, Rowdy placed his forefinger under her chin and tilted her head up to his. He kissed her lightly on the forehead, continuing down to the tip of her nose before capturing her lips. As his kiss deepened, he tightened his arms about her body pulling her closer to him. Her arms went around him. When the kiss ended, their breathing was erratic. He kissed her again then set her away from him and, whistling a tune, he headed to the barn.

Laura stood for some time in a daze. She had never been kissed before last night and now again this morning. She liked both men's kisses and the way they made her feel. *Should I have feelings about two men?*

Should I be kissing and loving on two men? She was beginning to understand what Jim had been trying to tell her last night. She might be pretty enough to catch the attention of a man. Now it seemed she had caught the attention of two men. She had forgotten, until now, how it felt to be young and interested in boys. She giggled. Jim and Rowdy were not boys, but men. And, as Jim had tried to explain to her, they had needs women did not. Or was that something Abner always drummed into her head? Yes, it was from him. She had wayward thoughts of her own. Was it possible to love two men? What happened if she did? She wished she could ask Cora about it. She knew about men. Didn't she?

As Laura did her chores, provoking daydreams tormented her. The two men complemented each other like night and day. Jim had thick, black, wavy hair; tanned skin; and beautiful dark blue eyes that lit up when he looked at her. He had a more serious side to his personality, unlike Rowdy, the jokester.

In so many ways Rowdy was his exact opposite. His blond hair, when wet, curled about his handsome face; the wind and the sun had darkened his skin to a golden hue. He was not as tall and lean as Jim, but his arms and legs were muscular. He often shared stories of working on the railroad as a youngster before the war. His green eyes always sparkled as if he was up to mischief, which matched his ever-present grin.

From the beginning, they'd treated her with the utmost kindness and respect. Did she want to lie with either as she had with Abner? She had never thought of lying with Abner as enjoyable. It was an ugly duty she had to perform. Never had she thought of lying with anyone else. Until now. Her guests were awakening feelings she had not known before. How could she control these feelings? Did she want to?

During the evening meals, she sensed a tenderness emerging from her for each of the men. She appreciated their presence, their jokes, and their compliments on her cooking.

That night after dinner, they carried their plates to the dishpan as usual. She'd long since given up protesting when they offered to help, welcoming their friendly jokes and company during the task.

Rowdy playfully grabbed Laura's hand in the hot dishwater, stroking it in a sensual manner then brushing her breast with his arm as he held her hand. While she tried to decide how to react, Jim pressed her into the counter, making her fully aware of his growing arousal. She was not only sweating from the hot water, but the hot attention they lavished on her.

It took longer to do the dishes that night. By the time the last pan was hung on its hook, Laura was breathing hard, sensual thoughts occupying her mind.

Jim stopped at the door without turning around, "We'll be gone most of the day tomorrow hunting. Will you fix us some trail grub to take along?"

"Yes, I'll fix each of you a grub sack, in case you are separated," she said sadly, already missing them.

The next day Laura waved good-bye as the men rode out at daybreak. No matter what they brought back, she would put it in the smokehouse and cure the meat to preserve it. What security and comfort they'd provided. But soon they would ride out of her life. She had seen the strange looks cross their faces when they stared off into the sky or stood searching the dark forests for ghosts from their past. They seldom spoke of what they'd suffered during the war, and when they did it was expressed with much grief. She allowed them their privacy. Sometimes a strangeness would come over Jim, and he frightened her. He would disappear into the forest and be gone for hours. When he returned, he was moody and did not want company.

Rowdy always seemed to have a bottle handy when his melancholy would come upon him. He would build a campfire on a hill, where he could drink and be alone with his ghosts.

As she watched them suffer in their quiet agonies, she did not want to tie either one down to a mortgaged ranch. It would not be good for her or the one who stayed. Besides she would never marry again and give someone total control over her being.

Many thoughts whirled through her mind as she toiled most of the morning in her garden. She had regained her strength since her accident and was thankful to do her own work again. She had left the milking to the men so she did not have to deal with the cow, but what would she do when they were gone? She would cross that bridge when she came to it. For now, her vegetables were growing fast as the warm springtime blossomed and before long, they would be able to enjoy them. The early corn had sprung up and was now putting on ears from stalks that towered over her head. Thinking of how delicious the fresh corn was going to be, she licked her lips in anticipation. Green beans were climbing the poles; carrots, radishes, and beets were already pushing their green leaves skyward. Early planting of onion slips had the bulbs already becoming the perfect size for eating. Canning time was drawing near, and she was ready for it. Each jar she put up was a promise she would survive the winter. The past winter had been mild, but she expected the coming one to be a bad one.

She had a good supply of butter to take to Everclear to trade for supplies. She would need Cora's and her girls' help to make it happen, hoping they would go with her when she had to meet Tuffy. Knowing Tuffy was mean and angry with her did not make the decision to go any easier and because there was no lawman in the mining town, she knew she was unsafe. The marshal would have to come from Denver when there was trouble. But she would soon be forced to go because she needed sugar, flour, and other basic items she could not grow or find in the forest. The cellar kept the eggs, milk, butter, and meat fresh until she could make a trip to town. She finished up her morning chores by churning butter from the milk and storing it in large crocks in the cellar.

As she worked, she thought of the Wilsons, who lived on the land joining hers on the west. They had not come to visit since last fall. Deciding to pack one of her last remaining smoked venison roasts, bread, butter, and milk; she wanted to see how they had fared during the winter months.

After her light lunch, Laura loaded the packsaddle and horse for her trip. Mrs. Wilson had told her once they came out several years ago from Virginia with their four children and then had another baby since arriving. Just like she and Abner, they had been unprepared for the harshness of living in the mountains with its severe winters and short growing season. Laura hoped they had learned to live with the rugged conditions.

Riding Beauty and leading the packhorse, she headed toward the main trail. Avoiding the hidden entrance to her place, she elected to wind her way through the trees to the lane leading to the Wilsons' cabin a little way off the main road. As soon as she drew near, she saw huge claw marks scratched into the front door. Since only a giant grizzly could have made the marks, she quickly pulled her rifle from its scabbard. Cautiously, she continued on to the dilapidated shack.

Yelling out, "Hello to the Wilsons!" she rode up to the front porch.

After a long pause, while she feared the worst, the door opened a crack and Mr. Wilson poked his head out. He peered left and right and then opened it the rest of the way, allowing his family to crowd outside.

"Hello, Mrs. Brown," Mr. Wilson greeted her sadly.

"Hello to you and your family," Laura answered, climbing down from Beauty. Her rifle rested in the crook of her arm as she held both horses' reins while she looked closely at the motley group before her. Mrs. Wilson's hair was wild and unkempt and the children faces and hands were smudged with dirt appearing to have not been washed in days. Mr. Wilson's clothes hung on him and looked as if he had lived in them for some time. The times Laura had seen him, he was always clean-shaven, but today he appeared as if he had not shaved in many days.

What could have happened to make this family look and act like this?

Concern for them showed as she said, "I came by to check on you since I have not seen you since last fall. Are you all right?" No one said anything as the group continued to stare at her.

Mr. Wilson coughed and leaned against the doorway. "We haven't had much to eat or drink lately."

Mrs. Wilson held the youngest child in her arms, but neither looked hearty. The other children had not fared much better either. The oldest boy, Matthew, who looked to be about sixteen, and his fourteen-year-old sister, Annie, had eyes that were sunk into their sockets and both looked as if they had been crying. Their cheeks were drawn and pale. The two younger children were hiding behind their mother's skirt and whimpering in fear continually looking around.

"If you will help me unload the packsaddle we can have some dinner." She reached for a saddlebag, but the group swarmed off the porch and whisked the food into the cabin and consumed it in a flash. Laura followed them in and stood in the doorway in disbelief. What could have happened to these people to cause them to act in such a manner?

"Please forgive us. We have not eaten in three days," explained Mr. Wilson as he wiped his dirty mouth on his sleeve.

"What has happened?" Laura asked.

"A grizzly has been terrorizing us for weeks. He was prowling around at night, but now he is lurking nearby in the daytime, too. He tore up the garden and killed our milk cow. I haven't been able to hunt because he follows and takes the kill. And I fear he might kill me instead. We are at our wit's end, Mrs. Brown." He wiped a tear from his cheek.

"Why don't you shoot him?" Laura asked.

"Well, I did, several weeks ago but I didn't kill him. I think it only made him mad. Whenever we go outside, he attacks. Did you see him when you rode up?"

"No, thank goodness. I better get going before it starts to get dark. He might try to follow me, too." She gathered up the empty baskets and milk pail and opened the door just wide enough to peek out. Not seeing the bear, she quickly loaded her items on the packhorse and climbed up on Beauty. "You should kill the bear before something bad happens. Bear meat is good and healthy. Then you would at least have something to eat for a while. You can't let him stop you from feeding your family." Laura waved good-bye to the family and rode hard toward the lane back to the main trail. Continuing to watch the trail and woods, she made her way back home. Relief washed over her when her cabin came into sight. She dug her heels into Beauty's side, and the horse galloped down the path to the river and then upward to her haven.

The Widow's Peak was what she secretly called the high point near her cabin. Of course, no one knew she was a widow, except for Jim and Rowdy. The Wilsons had not even asked about Abner. Oh well, one less couple she would have to lie to. She rode on to the barn to unsaddle and feed the horses.

Hurrying back to the cabin, she went inside, pulling the bar down to secure the door. Then she closed and barred all the shutters. Finally, she sat in her rocking chair and took a deep breath. Her trip to fulfill her Christian duty had been a good thing because she had been able to help the Wilsons at least for one day. However, their fear had transferred to her. She did not need to know a bear could wreak so much havoc on a family. *What if he comes over here? What would I do?* She rocked and thought about what she should do in the event of a bear attack.

Tamping down her fears, she lifted down the large buffalo rifle Tuffy had talked Abner into buying. Abner knew he was paying too much for it, but bought it anyway to save face. He never took it down from its hooks. Tomorrow, she would set up targets to make sure she was able to handle it. It was heavier than her rifle and she wanted to be prepared. She had learned quickly how to handle a rifle and a handgun when she first came to live in the wilderness. Just holding the big gun, she felt better. She had seen what fear had done to the Wilsons and it was not going to happen to her.

After cleaning the buffalo gun, she placed it back in its place on the wall with the other guns. The men would be back soon, so she started peeling potatoes to fry. Taking a smoked elk roast from the cellar, she began to slice it. With a pan of gravy and biscuits, it would be a filling supper. As she finished, she heard hoof beats.

Jim and Rowdy rode in, shouting. Opening the cabin door, she walked out on the porch, happy to see the men and the packhorses laden with meat.

"What did you get?"

Jim beamed. "Rowdy got a large elk, and I killed a deer. We got into a flock of turkeys and killed several. We have them gutted and will hang them in the trees to cool for the night. Supper ready?" A warm smile curved his lips as he looked at her.

"It's ready when you two get ready. Come on in after you wash up."

"We'll get these cooling and take care of the horses before we come in," yelled Rowdy as he threw a rope over a high limb in a tree.

When the men came in, they brought the livers and hearts, her favorite parts. She placed them in the root cellar to cool overnight. Tomorrow, she would prepare a delicious stew and fry up some of the liver.

Everyone was laughing and joking with each other. They were glad to be back with Laura even though they'd only been gone since morning. They could not resist touching her arm or shoulder whenever they passed. As they ate their meal, she told them about her neighbors. They scoffed when she said she had cleaned the buffalo gun getting it ready if she needed it.

"It's not funny that I want to protect myself," she fiercely reminded them.

"Laura, we laughed because the gun is so big and you're so small," said Rowdy.

"I'm a good shot, but I'll need to learn how to shoot the bigger gun."

"We know you can hunt for yourself if need be, and we're glad you can protect yourself when it is necessary," answered Jim as he gave her a special look.

Her heart melted from his look. "Anyone want a piece of pie?"

They answered together, "Yes!" and Laura got up to serve the pie.

After the dishes were washed and put away, they retired early. As Laura lay in bed in the darkness, her thoughts turned toward the two men again. Were they comfortable? Did they think of her at all? What would it be like to have one of them in her bed right now? *Oh my goodness.* She remembered how it was to have Abner on top of her. He'd never kissed her or even touched her in any way to make her want him. The memories of the night Jim had held her close came flooding over her. He was strong, lean, muscular and hard, his maleness pushing against her. He had said he wanted her. Did she want him like that? She was not sure what all of it meant. She had feelings for him and for Rowdy, too. But how could she choose between them?

She touched herself in ways she had never done before, discovering wetness between her legs. Continuing to experiment, she delighted herself with sensations she'd never before dreamed were possible. Had Jim and Rowdy ever thought of her in this way? She was innocent, as Jim had said, but she wanted to learn more about these new feelings. After she made her decision, she drifted off into a dreamless sleep.

CHAPTER 9

The next morning, Laura put on her work pants. Her few dresses were wearing out and she had reconstructed some of Abner's pants to fit her. They were much more convenient and easier to work in. She made a mental note to alter more of Abner's pants before she wore these out. The more her independence grew, the more she liked it.

Strapping her pistol and holster to her hip and picking up the rifle she had cleaned last night and the bag of shots and powder horn, she headed out to set up practice targets. When she had six cans lined up, she raised the monstrous rifle to take aim. She much preferred her smaller rifle, but she was determined to learn to use this one.

As she raised the buffalo rifle to her right shoulder, sighting down the long barrel, she thought she was prepared for the recoil, but she was mistaken. The explosion knocked her backward onto her butt and left her dazed for a moment from the recoil and the haze of smoke from the gunpowder circling her head. Her ears rang from the sound of the loud explosion.

When she got her wits back, she expected the can to be gone, but it was still sitting there. Glaring at it still sitting on the log made her even more determined. Getting up, she reloaded the rifle and took aim again. This time, braced for the recoil, she sent the can flying into the air. "Yahoo! I hit it!" Reloading and shooting the rest of the cans off the log one by one, she proved she could defend herself. *Just let that old bear come around here and he will be sorry.*

Loud whistles and clapping came from near the river where the men were boning and cutting up the animals they had killed the day before.

Laura bowed several times; proud they had watched her shoot. But she had her chores to do now and couldn't take any more time from her busy day. Glancing with anticipation at the two handsome men who were working with their shirts off again, she returned to the cabin.

Later, as they ate their evening meal, the men talked about Laura and the big gun.

"Laura, I do believe you can take care of yourself if need be," joked Rowdy but the mirth did not reach his eyes.

"I didn't have anyone to depend on but myself until you showed up. I've learned, since I've been living in this wild country, that I have to be prepared for whatever the land throws at me. I never want to be as the Wilsons are now. They are so frightened; they won't leave their cabin. I know they won't survive another winter out here if they don't change. I felt bad about not taking them more food, but it would jeopardize my survival if I continue to feed them. I will check on them soon, but I want Mr. Wilson to take care of the problem. Am I wrong to think this way?" she asked with tears in her eyes.

"You're supposed to help your neighbor, but they have to help themselves, too," agreed Jim.

"I know, but they seemed so helpless. I don't know what else to do."

It was late when they quit playing poker for the night. Laura rose from the table, wiping tears from her eyes because she had been laughing about something funny Jim had told on Rowdy.

Rowdy bent down and kissed Laura on the lips. "I had a wonderful time tonight. See you in the morning. Tell us what you want done tomorrow and we'll take care of it. Good night."

She managed to say, "Good night."

Jim leaned down and kissed her on the lips also. He whispered in her ear, "You taste like honey. Sweet dreams, Laura, darling." When the door closed behind him, Laura stood motionless for some time, touching her heated lips.

Sweet dreams! How could she dream when she was too keyed up to sleep? She lay in bed thinking of the two men in the lean-to who'd kissed her. She might ask one to stay, but which one? She cared for both. How could she choose?

Thinking of chores she could not do by herself got her mind off the men and their beautiful bodies and back onto more practical matters. She drifted off into a restless sleep where both Jim and Rowdy kissed her and touched her in special ways. Sweet dreams.

~

Laura had breakfast almost ready the next morning when the men came in. Pouring cups of coffee, they talked with Laura as she put the food on the table. After the blessing, they discussed what chores and repairs were needed. One major job she needed them to do was trim and shoe the horses' hooves. She requested repairs to the fence around the garden to prevent wildlife from eating her vegetables and work on the winter wood supply, too.

Jim and Rowdy spent most of the morning repairing the garden fence making it higher to keep out animals that would rob Laura of her precious vegetables. While they went off into the forest to drag in fallen trees to cut into firewood, she gathered the ingredients to bake their favorite apple pie for supper. She did not know any other way to repay them.

Laura slid the pie into the oven and returned to preparing and preserving the fresh meat and turkeys they had butchered.

Later in the evening, when they came back to the cabin, she placed baked potatoes, a large bowl of gravy, and fried liver on the table. When she joined them, they said the blessing. While they ate, Laura was unusually quiet. They attempted to get her to talk, but she would not respond with her happy chatter. Perhaps her sadness came from knowing they would be leaving soon. Their restlessness became more evident to her every day.

She rose and refilled each man's coffee cup. When she sat back down, she thanked Jim and Rowdy for all the work they had done for her.

"We've been helping each other. Remember? We needed a place to stay and you needed our help with repairs. So I think we're even," declared Rowdy.

Jim remained silent.

Tears rolled down Laura's cheeks. "There is no possible way I can ever repay you for all you have done to help me. I have nothing of value except the ranch, and it is mortgaged."

The men moved to kneel on either side of her, wiping her tears with their work-roughened hands, all the while making soothing sounds of comfort that touched her heart.

"Here now, woman! We wanted to help you. You fed us and gave us a place to sleep." Rowdy patted her shoulder.

"But I have nothing else to give you," Laura sobbed into her handkerchief.

"But you do," murmured Jim.

"What do you mean?"

"You could choose one of us to stay and take care of you. You know we care for you, and you can't do everything by yourself," Jim said tenderly.

Laura stared at him as if seeing him for the first time and said, "Oh, I could never choose between you. I care for both of you too much!"

"But, Laura, you have to choose one of us to stay and help you save the ranch," declared Rowdy.

Laura looked from one dear handsome face to the other as a thought began forming in her mind. "Why do I have to choose one? Why can't I have both of you?"

A loud silence followed her questions. Neither man moved or breathed. "Are you saying you would wed both of us?" Jim choked out.

She dropped her red face into her hands. "I don't want to wed anyone. Is it possible to bed both of you at the same time? One of Cora's girls said she did such a thing. I wondered how. Would it be fair to ask it of you?"

After a long moment, Jim asked, "Are you saying you want both of us at the same time or one of us one night and the other the next?"

"I don't know if it is possible for us to lie together at the same time, but, if so, you must agree to teach me what I am supposed to do to please each of you. We could learn together. But if you don't want to, I'll understand." Tears of shame splashed down her cheeks.

"Rowdy and I need to talk outside. We'll be right back." Taking Rowdy by the arm, Jim dragged him out onto the porch and closed the door.

Laura crept to the door and pressed her ear to the wood, anxious to hear what they might be discussing.

"What the hell are we going to do? I want her so bad but I don't want to share her with you or anybody," Jim said.

"Well, I feel the same way. Whoever wants to get married should ask her to marry him and stay here with her on the ranch," declared Rowdy nervously.

"I will ask her, and if she says yes, you will have to leave," replied Jim.

"I will ask her also, and if she says yes to me, you will have to leave," argued Rowdy.

When they went silent, she flew back to the table and resumed her seat.

They returned to kneel on either side of her chair. Rowdy grabbed her hand and asked in a loud voice, "Laura, will you marry me?"

"Rowdy, you are dear to me, but I have made a promise to myself never to marry again. Jim, I feel the same about you, but I will not marry either of you."

"But, Laura, we both care for you."

"That is why I cannot let this go on. I am beginning to learn about my needs and want both of you to teach me more. If you choose not to, I'll understand. But if we lie together, you have to promise me to leave soon after."

When they demanded to know why, she told them explicitly, "I was fifteen when I was forced into an unwanted marriage to an older man because of my parents' financial problems. I won't be forced into another marriage because I am alone with no money. I'm willing to sleep with both of you because I care for each of you, but I will not marry either of you."

They stared open-mouthed at her. When they did not quickly respond, she said, "If sleeping with me is so bad, then you can leave now."

"You don't understand; we want you so much, but we want you for ourselves. Will you spend one night with me, and the next with Rowdy?" Jim asked.

She stood up and began to pace and soon arrived at a decision "No. I am curious about what it means to make love to someone. You see, I want someone who cares about me to teach me how to love. I would like to learn from both of you—together. Is it too much to ask?"

"I would agree to anything to be able to kiss you and love you the way I have in my dreams," agreed Rowdy with emotion in his voice.

Both faced Jim who asked in a low voice, "When?"

"We'll plan on tomorrow night with the understanding that after we spent the night together, you will have no bonds on me and I will have no bonds on you. Agreed?" They nodded, kissing her on each cheek as they left the room without another word.

"What have I done?" Laura held her hot face. Taught to be chaste and pure, she read her Bible daily and had learned sleeping with anyone except a husband was sinful. However, life in the wilderness had a way of dealing from the bottom of the deck, forcing one to adjust to situations or die. Was this a do-or-die situation? She would ponder on that.

While she finished cleaning the kitchen, she began to think about what would happen after supper tomorrow night. All she had to do was lie there, and they would do all the work. That should be simple enough. A man got his pleasure once, and that was it. At least that was what had happened with Abner. Would these men be any different? Her feelings for them had caused her to make a stupid decision. Her fears of having someone rule over her again kept her from wanting to ever marry again. When they left, no one would ever know what she had done. Simple enough. Tonight she would write in her journal about the agreement. But what would she write about tomorrow night?

CHAPTER 10

*L*aura woke refreshed from a wonderful night's sleep. The night before, after she'd finished writing in her journal, she had set her mind at ease about the coming night. She had been able to sleep.

Laura outdid herself at breakfast with huge biscuits, gravy, fried eggs, bacon, and lots of coffee. She was happy. They shared breakfast as if it was a normal day, but she could tell Rowdy and Jim were extremely nervous about the coming night. Their nervousness endeared them more to her. She tried not to think of the coming night as well, but...when her gaze fell on one of them she could not help but wonder what the night would bring.

The men worked twice as hard to complete the chores Laura needed for them to finish. She'd asked them to lay in a good supply of firewood for the winter. She watched as they used their horses to drag in more dry trees from the forest to be cut into small logs and kindling. She worked to help out as much as possible while completing her own chores as well.

At about four o'clock, Laura suggested they quit and go relax and bathe in the river.

Jim and Rowdy headed for the river with scented lye soap Laura had made, towels, and their clean clothes while Laura went to the cabin to warm water for her bath. She needed time to bathe and wash her hair.

She left her long blonde hair down to dry as she prepared the evening meal. When the men came in, they gaped at her. She'd never worn her hair any way but braided. Tossing her head, she preened under their approval as their eyes widened and so did the bulges in their pants.

Too excited to wait any longer, Laura asked, "Are you ready to begin? What do you want me to do first?"

Jim spilled his coffee on the table, and Rowdy dropped his fork on his metal plate. Jim looked up. "I, uh, I suppose the first thing we need to do is put your mattress on the floor before the fireplace. I don't think your bed frame could support all of our weight."

She followed them as they carried the corn shuck mattress over in front of the fireplace. Kneeling, she straightened the covers. "Now what do we do?" she asked.

"We will leave the cabin for a while so you can get undressed and under the covers," croaked Jim as he and Rowdy turned heading for the door.

Nervously removing her dress and underclothes, Laura stood naked in the middle of the cabin, the cool air raising goose bumps on her bare skin. Slipping between the covers, she heard the door of the cabin open, sounds of feet shuffling in, and the whisper of clothes being removed. Then bare feet padding around to each side of the mattress. Laura, lying in the middle of the mattress, squeezed her eyes shut so she would not see the naked men. Their warm bodies touched her on each side as they slid in next to her. No one moved, as they lay there barely breathing.

Laura heard the rustle of the covers and felt their bodies turning toward her. "Laura open your eyes and look at us," Jim whispered.

"We want you to feel comfortable and unafraid," said Rowdy in a warm caring voice.

In the glow from the fireplace she could see each handsome man hovering over her. "Will you show me how it feels to be loved?"

Jim kissed her tenderly on the mouth. She shivered. He drew back. "Have you ever been kissed in bed?"

She shook her head.

Rowdy lifted her left breast and fondled the nipple, "Did your husband ever do this to you?"

She shook her head again.

"But I do like it," she whispered.

Jim claimed her mouth again while Rowdy continued to fondle, kiss, and nibble on her nipple drawing it into his hot mouth. She moaned in pleasure. The unfamiliar feelings burned a path down into her belly.

Jim kissed a trail of hot kisses from her earlobes down her neck to her other nipple where he lapped it with his tongue until it had peaked. He then began to tenderly bite and draw on it. Laura felt as if flames were consuming her. She arched her back, lifting her breasts to them, and begged for more. They touched her everywhere as she writhed.

Jim kissed his way down her hot body while Rowdy kissed her on his way upward, claiming her willing mouth with his tongue. Unsure at first, she soon began to enjoy it, and when she tongued him back, he placed her hand on his large, thick penis.

Never having touched a man before, she wanted to see what it looked like. But now all she did was run her palm up and down his stiff shaft. Rowdy moaned pushing back and forth. Just as she began to focus on Rowdy, Jim began kissing her between her legs. *What is he doing? Is that possible? Oh yes!* Crying out in rapture, she forgot everything but the moment. She felt like cream rising to the top of milk. Enjoying every sensation as it continued to build. It felt like she would explode, but how could she? Something wonderful was happening to her. She thrashed about, lost in the most wonderful feelings.

Rowdy was kissing her body and sucking on each of her breasts as Jim continued worshipping her secret place with his magical tongue. It did not take long before her wanton abandon caused her to shudder and beg them for more. As she urged him on with her bucking and cries, Jim continued to tenderly ravage her as he pushed his tongue in and out until she screamed out her release. "Yes! Yes! Yes! Don't stop!"

As she began to weep, they tenderly hugged her.

Jim and Rowdy sat up, while she came down from her sexual high. She stretched before them, glowing, experiencing the most wonderful sensations of her life. This was nothing like the horror she'd experienced when Abner raped her on her wedding night. This was caring, sensual, and so enjoyable. Shy, she wanted to know more about what had happened to her.

"You've never experienced a release like this before?" as Jim leaned over and kissed her again between her legs.

"No. My husband crawled on, rode me, yelled some, and crawled off. I thought that was all there was. I didn't know I was supposed to enjoy it, too."

"But you told us you had been married for five years," Rowdy said. "Did he not want you to respond to him in that way?"

"Once I felt something and began to move under him. He told me not to act like a whore, so I stopped. Was I wrong to do that?" Shame filled her at what she had admitted.

Rowdy exploded. "It was wrong of him not to let you seek your release as well. I can't believe a man would do that. You could've given him so much, but he didn't allow it."

They kissed her face and mouth, taking turns as they worked their way down to her breasts again. Jim placed his hard penis in her hand, as Rowdy had done. She gripped it tightly. Emboldened, she asked, "May I see you both? I've never seen a naked man before."

They proudly knelt, presenting themselves for her inspection. She moved closer. "They are different, yet alike. May I touch them?"

They nodded.

As she fondled both, the men each gave a strangled cry. She stopped. "Have I hurt you?"

"Oh no, your touch feels wonderful." Rowdy moved back and forth in her hand.

She continued stroking watching how their penises responded to her movements.

"Our concern about loving you is you will be with child from one of us," Jim said.

"You have nothing to worry about. I'm barren. Abner had other children, but I never could conceive. He was always angry with me because I couldn't." *She'd never thought to have to expose her shame so openly.*

"Please don't be sad. Let us make you forget the past and enjoy the present." Jim lowered her back to the mattress and spread her legs with his knees.

Rowdy moved aside.

Jim kissed her as he moved slowly downward. Feeling him pushing at her entrance she asked, "Will all of you go in?"

He reassured her. "I am pretty sure it will if we take it nice and slow." He kissed her passionately, pushing gently into her softness with his unyielding rod. She moaned at the pleasure. He stopped moving and whispered in her ear, "You're so tight I feel as if no one has been here before me."

"My husband was old and it didn't stay hard for long, but he did take my maidenhead on our wedding night. Yes, I have been bedded."

"But, Laura, have you ever been made to want it?" Jim pushed his way deeper into her. He began the dance of love with her. "Put your legs around me and move back and forth with me."

"Am I doing this right, Jim?"

"Oh honey, you are doing it so right."

Laura continued as he had instructed her and soon she was not able to control her body or her yelling as she climaxed again and again. Jim followed close behind her. Watching her reactions to his lovemaking.

As she began to return to earth after the swirl of their lovemaking, she looked around and asked, "Where did Rowdy go?"

"He left quietly so we could have some time alone."

After a while, Rowdy returned and lay down by Laura whose breathing had returned to normal. She placed her hand in his and waited for him to make the next move. Jim lay on the other side. Rowdy turned toward Laura and stroked her face. He began to kiss her waiting lips. Jim stroked her breasts, helping to build the fire in her again.

Rowdy threw his leg over her hip, pulling her to her side and closer to him. It didn't take long before she encircled his hardness and began stroking it.

As he pushed her to her back, she waited to see what would happen next. Laura could hear his rapid breaths or was that hers? Rowdy rose up spreading her legs with his knees as he lowered himself toward her welcoming body. As he did so, Jim slipped out of the cabin, allowing them their privacy as Rowdy had done.

Rowdy whispered, "I will be gentle," then continued to kiss her sweet lips and ease himself into her. She moaned her pleasure as she welcomed him in, moving as Jim had shown her.

Jim's penis was long and hard but Rowdy's was thicker and more muscular. It did not ease into her as Jim's had. But he taught her how to enjoy a new experience as she worked him in. Because of his thickness, it required more effort on her part, and she was a most willing helper.

She heard him moan his pleasure at her actions because she wanted him. She helped him gain entrance as they both fought for control. He continued to sink into her, as he whispered, "Does it feel as good to you as it does to me?"

Nodding, she pushed her hips upward, "Am I doing this right?"

"Oh baby, you are," he groaned. "I can die happy now." He continued his rocking motions slowly at first.

For a time, their lovemaking was steady and unhurried. His breathing accelerated. He cried out in his passion, "Come on, baby! Move your sweet ass and love me with all you got," as his pace sped up and he rode her harder. Frantic for her own release, she matched her hip actions with his.

Laura reached for the exploding stars then floated on clouds and drifted back to earth. Rowdy cried out in the throes of passion as his release filled her. They lay joined, breathing hard. Laura could not believe the emotions these two wonderful men had created in her. Knowing now what she had been missing made it even harder to think about them leaving.

When Jim returned, the three sat on the mattress talking. Laura surprised them with a special cake she had made for the occasion. As they drank coffee and ate the scrumptious dessert, she was embarrassed at first to sit naked before the men. But she realized after what they had shared it should not matter. Rowdy took icing from his slice of the cake, spreading it on one of her nipples. Laura giggled as he leaned over to lick it off with his hot tongue. Wanton for more, she stretched forward so he could easily reach her and enjoyed the love play.

Jim bent close and they licked and fondled her breasts with their tongues as they spread more icing on her.

Rowdy asked her in a lusty tone, "Do you like it?"

Blushing from head to toe, she said, "Oh, yes."

Their laughter filled the cabin, as the men returned to eating their cake, gazing at her as if she was next on the menu. They would leave soon, but they had taught her how to love.

When they finished their refreshments, they lay back down on the mattress looking at her. "Aren't we through?"

Dragging her hungrily down between them, Rowdy said, "Not by a long shot!"

"You mean there is more we can do?"

Rowdy chuckled. "Honey, we are going to teach you many ways of loving before the sun comes up tomorrow. Are you ready for lesson two?"

She looked from one naked man to the other as she began to stroke each hardening penis. "What's next?"

~

Short naps and more lovemaking continued throughout the night. The men showed her what it meant to be loved. She learned different positions, even how to make love to two men at the same time. But most importantly, they showed her how to enjoy pleasure and to give it, which was something she had never known.

The crowing of the rooster woke them. The naked men jumped up, hurrying to the door to retrieve their clothes and boots before leaving the cabin. Laura sat up watching them with amusement, no longer embarrassed by the sight of nudity. Their bodies were beautiful to her. But Jim and Rowdy behaved as if they had been caught doing something naughty. She did not feel the least bit guilty about what she had done. She had needs just as a man did. They had awakened her from her virginal sleep. She stretched and yawned like a cat as she began to warm water for a quick bath before starting breakfast.

What would they do, if I served breakfast in the nude? She giggled at her daring idea. They would not be back until she rang the breakfast bell. She warmed water and sponged her skin clean of the night's sweat, knowing the farewells were coming.

CHAPTER 11

*E*arlier today, Rowdy and Jim had saddled their horses and tied on their bedrolls and the provisions she had prepared for them. She hated good-byes, especially one as emotional as this.

Jim took her in his arms, giving her a letter proclaiming his love for her and telling her where she could find him in Texas if she ever needed him. Refusing to cry, she kissed him passionately. He clung to her before he released her, mounted his horse, riding a short distance away.

Rowdy had prepared a letter for her as well. He handed it to her and pulled her into his arms. "Please let me stay and be your husband and lover," he pleaded as he kissed her face before settling on her quivering lips.

"I can't, Rowdy. Maybe someday, but not now. I don't want to choose between you. Please try to understand," she whispered, hugging him for the last time.

Rowdy claimed her lips as if he were a dying man, kissing her with memories of last night. "At least my kiss will be the last on your lips today," he said swinging up onto his horse.

When they reached the top of the trail, on the other side of the valley, they waved back at her before disappearing from sight.

Laura sat on her bench near the cabin, overlooking her river valley. Unknown to her, Jim had secretly carved letters into her log bench. The letters formed the word "Forever" surrounded by a heart. She knew she would never forget the two angel men that had ridden into and out of her life. She would daydream about them "Forever." The large rise to the right of the cabin gave her a spectacular view of her ranch. Sitting here now, she thought of all that had happened to her since she came to live in the mountains. And she grew sad and fearful now that she was alone. Why did she force them to leave? She knew why, but still it gave her little comfort to know she loved two men who she forced to leave because she would not marry again. She wanted to choose her own destiny. Even if it meant she was alone.

She drew her knees up, wrapped her arms around them, and cried as she had never cried before. Terrible sadness came pouring out. She cried for all the wrongs done to her. She cried because she missed her family. She cried because she was isolated and alone. She cried because she was frightened of the unknown. She cried because she did not know what to do next since she had no money and no way of getting any. Her tears and sobs were deep wounds of grief, sadness, and even terror. Her sobs finally began to subside to silent tears and an occasional whimper.

Something warm brushed her arm. She was terrified. She had left her guns in the cabin and she had no protection. She could not breathe, knowing a wild animal had come to her. Whatever it was came to the sound she had been making. But the sound the intruder heard was her sadness pouring out. The animal rubbed her arm again with its fur and whimpered low.

Raising her head, she cried out when she saw the wolf, "Silver! You scared me to death!" She was thankful it was him. "We have a special bond, don't we?"

The large silver-colored timber wolf sat on his haunches, staring at Laura with his blue eyes. Small black markings around his head and eyes gave him a fearsome appearance, but now he was caring and docile with Laura. A reassuring sensation came from him that all would be well for her. He rose and came toward her, stopping to sniff and nudge her hand. She raised it, and petted his smooth soft fur before he turned and disappeared into the forest.

Her self-indulgence at an end, she took a deep breath, and set her mind on what she had to do to survive. Standing up she went into the cabin, strapped on her gun and holster before she went to the barn to begin her daily chores.

~

Seven nights after the men had left, a violent spring thunderstorm swept down from the mountains laden with heavy rain, booming thunder, and high winds. It continued through most of the night, lightning streaking across the sky for hours. The cabin shook when it thundered. She covered her head with the bed covers as if they would protect her if the roof caved in on her in the deluge.

Nevertheless, she survived until morning. Daylight revealed broken limbs and several large trees down. The small stream from the spring on the mountain ridge high above her grassy meadow flowed stronger and faster now. She needed to check it out when she could get up there. She would have to wait until the sun dried the trail enough to make the hike. Heavy flooding had caused the river to rise dangerously close to the barn, but the cabin was not in danger.

Days later, while pulling weeds and gathering some of the early vegetables, the odor of her sweaty body became overwhelming. She could use a bath. She did not want to haul several buckets of water and then wait for it to heat. What else could she do? *Why not bathe in the spring?* She needed to check it out anyway. She returned to the cabin for clean clothes, soap, and a cotton cloth to dry off with. Since the thunderstorm and heavy rain several days ago, the weather had become hot and humid. A bath in the cold spring would be invigorating.

Laura followed the stream across the large grassy meadow. She liked the protection the edge offered high above her, dotted with tall green pines and beautiful aspens with white bark and black knots.

When she reached the waterfall near the top of the rim, she discovered the storm had reshaped and deepened the small pool enough so she now could stand under the waterfall to wash her hair.

After removing her clothes, she stepped into the cold spring, enjoying the sensation of being nude in the great outdoors. Moving under the overhang, she felt the icy tentacles wrap around her warm body as it circled her like a giant spider web. At the first touch of the freezing water, she sucked in her breath and held it, then released it with a pleasure filled giggle. Why had she waited so long to enjoy such a simple pleasure?. Her nipples perked, reddening from the sensation of the cool water. As she stood there, washing her hair, something hard hit the top of her head. She yelped with pain as the offending object splashed into the water at her feet. Bending over, she picked up a large, shiny golden rock and turned it over in her hand. What could it be? Some of the sides were shiny and flat, and others were sharp and uneven. Could this be a gold nugget, something she had heard so much about but had never seen before?

She searched in the pool for more. Sure enough, she found another one. Picking it up, she followed the stream. The late afternoon sun threw slanting light across the grassy meadow.

Laura walked along, picking up golden rocks. Finally, she held all she could manage. She laid the sparkling stones down near her clothes, stepped back into the icy water to finish bathing. Picking up her clothes and the rocks, she walked nude down the path to the cabin. *There is nothing like the freedom without clothes,* she thought as she strolled down the path. Suddenly hearing a sound high above her, she stopped to stare up into the mountains. She whistled for Silver thinking it may have been him. Sensing eyes on her nude body, she turned hurrying with Silver to the cabin.

~

Eagle Talon, a Southern Ute medicine man, nudged his beautiful stud, Spotted Horse, deeper into the aspen trees, staring at the water spirit in the spring. Her glowing white body glistened as water droplets ran down her shapely nude back. Her long, straw-colored hair waved in the soft breeze as if beckoning to him. Could this be a mystical spirit he happened upon to help him with his buffalo quest? Or was it an evil spirit sent to lead him away from his search? He was unsure which as he continued to stare at the beautiful woman's nude body, afraid to stay and afraid to go.

Spotted Horse whinnied as the spirit walked away. She stopped, turning to stare in the direction of the sound. Eagle Talon gasped when the spirit turned its nude body toward him. Clutching clothes in her right arm, the large right breast was concealed, but the other stood out, pointed and exposed to his view. His eyes traveled the full length of the spirit's body, unfamiliar with the straw colored thatch of hair between her legs. Indian women were dark haired and dark skinned. Comparing the differences, he was intrigued to find out more about this spirit if he could.

The horse and rider blended into the forest. They did not move. The only sounds heard were those of the small cascading waterfall and the forest leaves quaking in the soft breeze.

As he watched, the spirit gave a loud whistle and waited. From the edge of the forest above where the water spirit had been bathing, a large silver wolf appeared and made his way down to her side. The vision stroked his fur and said something to him. Then the spirit and wolf turned, going down the path to the cabin and disappearing from view into the line of trees.

After the water spirit and wolf disappeared from view, Eagle Talon continued to think about what he had witnessed. The horse stomped his impatience to go, but still the medicine man did not give the horse the signal. He replayed the vision in his mind. He was more afraid now because the being had called to a timber wolf, which had obeyed its command. Now he wondered if it was a "Wolf Woman" or "She Who Speaks to Wolves." It had called to his spirit as well as the animals that responded to her. He would have to be careful and watch this spirit.

When he touched Spotted Horse with his knees to go, he realized his body had responded with desire to the vision. *Did he desire a Spirit Woman? What would happen to him if he touched her? What had the Spirit Woman done to him?* He would seek counsel from his spirit guides to know if it was a good spirit or an evil one.

~

Laura hid the rocks in a basket in the cellar. Taking a bucket the next morning, she climbed to the top of the rim above the spring. She wanted to discover the source of the nuggets. The savage storm had uprooted a large pine tree growing on the edge of the stream. Golden rocks like decorations on a Christmas tree clung to the root ball. What she'd found before was nothing compared to the potential wealth to be picked up. But was it gold or the notorious fool's gold Abner told her had tricked many a miner?

As she gathered the nuggets, she whispered prayers of thanksgiving to the Lord for again taking care of her needs. If these were gold nuggets, she would have enough money to secure her land, and perhaps enough to live on. She made a number of trips to the cabin to hide the buckets of nuggets before she settled her nerves enough to do her chores for the day.

How could she find out if they were real without causing an uproar? She had heard stories while on the wagon train of how men went crazy during gold strikes. When she crawled into bed that night, sore from carrying heavy buckets and climbing up and down the rocky trail, a plan began to emerge she hoped would work.

CHAPTER 12

*L*aura settled into the saddle, shivering, as the sun peeked over the mountains. Even in late May, it would be hours before the day's warmth pushed aside the high-altitude chill. She tugged on the packhorse's rope, anxious to get to Cora's with her gifts of eggs and butter. She had packed the baskets with straw to protect the eggs from breaking, putting the crocks of butter into a separate basket. She had brought extra to trade with Tuffy to cover her real reason for riding into town. She had to find out if the nuggets were real.

By mid-morning, she had reached the creek a half mile from the settlement. While the horses drank their fill, she waded in the creek several times bending to pick up rocks to examine. None held the sparkling yellow metal of those in her spring. She put several rocks from the creek bed into her pocket. Then scattering small golden nuggets into the spring, she put her plan into action.

It was still too early for Cora and the girls to be up, but Laura pounded on the door until Cora welcomed her, wearing a flimsy robe in a floral pattern. "I am so glad to see you," Cora said, throwing her arms around Laura. "Are you coming back to work for me? We miss your cooking."

"I brought you fresh eggs and butter for your biscuits. And I need your help. Will you send Hank out to get the baskets?"

Cora yelled for Hank before turning back to Laura. "What do you want me to do? I'm happy to help you." She ushered her into the kitchen to pour Laura some coffee.

"I need supplies. I brought eggs and butter to trade with Tuffy, if he will do it. However, I am afraid to go in there alone. I hoped you and the girls would accompany me to the trading post when I confront him. Also, I have found something—I am not sure what it is." Laura laid out two small gold nuggets on the table before Cora. "Do you know what these are?" she asked innocently.

Cora picked the nuggets up, staring at them, then at Laura. "Girl, these look like pure gold. Where did you find them?"

"I stopped down at the stream to water the horses before I got to town. I saw something gleaming in the water and picked these up. Do you think they are gold? Is it that easy to find gold?"

Cora sputtered. "They look like the real thing, but Tuffy will know if they are. We will get dressed and come with you. I understand why you would be afraid to go in the lion's den without us."

Laura sipped coffee and tried to steady her nerves while she waited until the ladies were dressed. Cora brought Hank with them as well. They strolled down the street toward the trading post, with Laura nervously leading her horses behind them. She was afraid, but had no other way to find out about the gold. And with Cora and the girls at her side, perhaps she would be safe. When they reached the trading post, Hank carried the remaining baskets inside.

As Laura entered, Tuffy begin to spew his venom at her. "Well, if it's not Mrs. Brown and the rest of the whores. Come to beg me for more supplies? Or do you need a real man yet?"

"Good day to you, Mr. Sawyer," Laura replied. "I brought fresh eggs and butter to barter with you today for some supplies. Are you willing to do that?" She glanced about the post to see how many were in there to witness what was about to take place.

"I knew you would be back begging me to help you, even though you resisted me before," he sneered.

Laura raised her voice so all could hear. "If you think I am here to beg for anything, you are sadly mistaken. I have brought eggs and butter to barter because this is a trading post, isn't it? Do you want my business or not? How long would you be in business if no one came in here?"

Tuffy's face turned bright red. "All right, let's see what you brought."

Hank placed the baskets on the counter. Tuffy looked through each one before Laura handed him her list. He grumbled as he walked off to fill it.

When he returned, he began to add the supplies up. Grabbing a stub of a pencil and a piece of brown wrapping paper, Laura began noting all the supplies and adding up the figures. "What are you doing?" Tuffy roared.

"I am adding the amounts of what I brought and subtracting it from the total of the goods I got from you," she replied.

"Do you think I would cheat you?"

She stared at him long enough he knew the answer to his question. "Abner entrusted me to come to town with what little we have. I want to make sure I do it right."

Muttering under his breath about prissy women, Tuffy continued adding the columns until they both agreed on the total.

When they finished, Hank headed outside to load her purchases on her packhorse.

Tuffy asked, "So when do I get the ranch? We all know you and Abner will lose it because you can't make the payment."

Laura gave him a level stare. "Can you show me the books and how much we owe you? The full balance."

He opened the account book "I don't know why Abner doesn't take care of his own business instead of letting a female do it for him."

Tuffy showed Laura their total.

She reached into her pocket and laid two rocks on the counter. "Are these worth anything?" Tuffy held them, turned them over, and laughing at her said. "These are worthless river rocks."

"Well, what about these," she asked quietly as she laid the two gold nuggets down in front of him.

The silence in the room was deafening as Tuffy and nearby customers stared at the golden nuggets. The others moved closer. Tuffy gaped at the larger nugget and then at the smaller one. "Where did you find these?"

"I want to know how much for them. Then I will tell you." Laura motioned for Cora to come closer.

"I will have to test and weigh them before I know." He glared at her and then Cora.

"I'll wait."

He scurried over to his chemicals for testing ore and his scales. Weighing each one, he wrote down some figures. Laura watched him closely as he rubbed one of the nuggets on black cloth, leaving a golden smear. When he dripped a few drops of cyanide on it, the smear began to dissolve. As he turned around, he almost ran over her in his haste and excitement. "These are almost pure gold. Where did Abner find them? Are there more?" He asked as he slipped the nuggets into his coat pocket.

"How much, Tuffy?" Laura asked loudly.

Blowing out a sigh, he said, "Enough to pay your debt with lots left over."

Laura cast Cora a pleased grin. "Do you have enough money to pay me the difference?"

"Let me give you credit for the difference."

"No, I want the money, and I want it today. If you can't pay me then I will take the nuggets and go to Denver. I will pay you what I owe you when I return."

Hatred flamed in his eyes. "Can you give me until the afternoon? I'll have your money then."

"Well, I'll wait until just after lunch. Give me the nuggets and when I return, we will close our deal." She eyed him. "In case you've forgotten, they're in your pocket."

Angrily throwing the nuggets down on the counter in front of her, he stalked away from her.

Laura and the other women rushed outside excitedly. Laura had bested Tuffy at his own game. Now they returned to Cora's to celebrate. But Hank slipped into the woods behind the trading post to keep an eye on Tuffy.

Settling into a seat in Cora's dining room, Laura couldn't believe how her luck had changed. "I couldn't have managed without all of you. Thank you so much." Tears of joy and relief washed over her.

As they set plates of bread and cheese on the table, Hank returned to tell the women he'd watched Tuffy sweating and cursing as he dug up money he had buried.

After they had eaten, they returned to the trading post where a crowd had gathered. From the cheerful comments thrown their way, word had spread about the gold and about a woman getting the best of Tuffy Sawyer.

Tuffy gave Laura a hateful glare as she approached him.

She ignored his attitude. "Are you ready to complete our deal?"

Biting hard on his stinking cigar, he said, "I have the rest of your money if that is what you are asking."

"I want to see the books and our account marked paid in full. Then I want you to give me a receipt and the balance in cash."

"Where are the nuggets?" he bit out.

Placing them on the counter, she was careful not to touch his greedy hands.

When the transaction had been completed and her ranch safe and secure, Tuffy demanded the location of the find.

"Oh, it's an interesting story. This morning, I stopped at the creek outside of the settlement to water the horses. That's when I saw the shiny rocks. I wondered if they could be gold."

"Are there any more?" Tuffy demanded.

"If I had seen any more, don't you think I would have picked them up, too?"

Suddenly, the wood floor rumbled under the stampede of the crowd out the front door. Only she and her friends and a red-faced Tuffy remained.

"You will be sorry for this, you damn bitch," Tuffy yelled. She had no doubt he would get even with her if he could.

The women and Hank hurried out of the trading post back to Cora's where Laura had left her horses. Hugs and kisses were exchanged before Laura mounted her horse and, trailing her packhorse, waved good-bye to Cora and the girls.

"Come back to see us real soon," Cora yelled.

As she crossed the creek where she had planted the gold, men were already panning for gold. She heard one shout, "I found a nugget!" She grinned.

It had been an eventful day with everything going her way. The money from the two nuggets was a small fortune, and she had so many more, she could take care of herself for the rest of her life. She was no longer a pauper.

When she reached her cabin late in the evening, the shadows were growing longer. She had been careful to watch her trail as she came home, since everyone in town knew she carried money. She unloaded the pack-horse and grabbed the lantern then took the horses to the barn to feed them. As soon as she locked up the chickens, she hurried for the security of her cabin. Bolting the door and then the shutters on the windows, she let out a loud yell of happiness and relief. After putting away her supplies, she sat down at the table to count her money. But what was she to do about the rest of her treasure-trove? What could she do with them? She could not go back to Tuffy with more. She sat for a long time deep in thought.

When she went to bed, she said her prayers thanking the Lord for helping her and asking Him to continue to guide her in making the right decisions about the new wealth He had given her. She went to sleep hugging the paid-off ranch receipt and dreaming of Jim and Rowdy.

CHAPTER 13

*T*he next morning beamed bright and sunny and so did Laura's mood. She had not seen or heard from the Wilsons since she last visited. Hoping the problem they were having with the bear had been resolved, she saddled her mare and loaded the packhorse with some extra supplies. The family was probably out of basics like sugar, flour, canned goods, fresh eggs, and butter. She had been careful with her meat supply since the men had left, but if the Wilsons needed anything it would be meat. Taking a freshly cured elk ham from the smoke house, she packed it in with all the other supplies.

Nearing the cabin an hour later, she called out, "Hello in the cabin!" She did not see any activity, and the place appeared deserted. The door opened a crack and a weak voice called out, "Who is it?"

Laura dismounted. "Matthew? Is that you? I have come by to check on you all and to bring you some supplies. Please come out."

The youth and his two younger sisters emerged onto the porch, peering around nervously. How drawn they were. "When have you last eaten?"

Shaking his head, he blushed. "The bear killed my pa several weeks ago when he went out to hunt for us. It tracked him down and got him. We heard him yelling but we were too afraid to go out of the cabin to help." Tears ran down his face. The two little girls began to cry, too.

"I am sorry for your loss. Has the bear continued to come back?" She glanced anxiously around her.

"No, ma'am. We have not seen or heard him since he killed Pa."

"If you'll help me with the supplies, I will make you something to eat." She laid her long rifle over her arms and stood guard while he carried the food into the cabin. Just because the bear hadn't been back in a while didn't mean he wouldn't show up, especially when she was unloading food.

Inside the cabin, the overpowering smell of unwashed bodies, feces, urine, and fear assailed her. Fear had a powerful odor as well as being contagious.

Their mother lay on the dirty bed with the youngest child suckling at her breast. Her nipples were bleeding from the child's attempts to nurse. It was apparent she had not had any water or nourishment for some time. Her face was pale and her eyes closed, sunken as if she were dying.

Laura began giving orders. "I will have you all something to eat soon but you have to help me help you. I cannot do it by myself. Do you understand?" She stared into the eyes of each child. Knowing the mother would be of no help, she asked Matthew to take the other children outside to bring fresh water from the spring.

"You want us to go outside so the bear can eat us too?" Matthew squeaked.

Laura would have to take a different approach. Picking up her long rifle, she laid it across her arms. "This is my bear gun. I keep all bears away from my place with it, and I can do the same thing here. It is big and loud, and it brings down a bear anytime I aim it at one. I will be watching you with it cocked and ready. Do you understand?"

The children bolted for the door, seeming to be more frightened of her than the bear, except for the youngest little girl who came back to Laura, motioning for her to lean down. Laura knelt and the girl whispered, "Are you an angel?"

"The Lord hears our prayers and always sends someone to help in our darkest hours. I have been sent here to help you and your family," replied Laura, remembering when she had a visit from two special angels on horses.

She turned to the other children, who lingered inside the door. "I didn't bring any food prepared to eat, so I will have to cook it. I need lots of water hauled from the spring to clean the pots and dishes before I can begin. I will need wood as well. Will you all help me? I will be watching you with my bear gun from the porch as you bring the buckets of water. Okay?" They nodded, then darted outside and grabbed the buckets stacked on the porch.

She stood on the porch waiting with her gun as each child carried a bucket of water inside. She gave the children a drink of fresh water as their mother noticed Laura for the first time. She beamed as if she had seen an angel also, as she mouthed to Laura, "thank you." Laura nodded.

Soon, she had water heating and the frying pan scrubbed. She filled it with bacon, set coffee to boil and slid a tray of biscuits into the oven. With Laura's insistence, Matthew had gotten brave enough to go to the woodpile for more wood and he began to help Laura. When the biscuits were almost ready, she scrambled a dozen eggs and asked the children to please wash up for the meal. They stood motionless, gazing in horror at Laura, as if she had grown horns.

"What's the matter?" Laura asked.

"We ain't done that in a long time. We just want to eat now," said the middle girl.

"Well, you and your family will not get a bite of food until you wash up and wash up well," said Laura in a loud and commanding voice.

The children ran for the water bucket to wash their faces and hands and smooth back their hair. When they returned to the table, Laura grinned sweetly at them to let them know they pleased her.

"Please be seated, but I will serve you a little at first. I do not want you to eat too fast. It will make you sick. I know it will be hard to do but you are all strong and very brave. See what you have done today to help your family? I will say a blessing for the food and pray for your family to heal from its grief over your pa's death. Bow your heads now."

After she had served the children, she took a plate of food to their mother, who had not moved from the bed. Helping her to sit up, Laura fed her a bite at a time. She continued to make her drink water to replenish her body. Mrs. Wilson fell asleep before she had finished the last of the eggs.

When Laura returned to the table, the children had eaten all their food and begged for more. "I will give you more if you drink your cups of water first." Then she gave them a bit more food, encouraging them again to eat slowly so they would not get sick.

After they had eaten, they seemed more energetic. She asked Matthew to get more water because she wanted to start a stew cooking for supper. He jumped up to do it, but refused to go out without her on the porch with her gun. She agreed. He managed to carry two buckets of water by himself. "I'm proud of you for helping your family." He beamed.

When she had the water and meat in the large stew pot heating in the fireplace, she told the children they would accompany her to their garden. She could see the fear of going outside again written on their faces. Picking up her bear gun, she opened the door for them. They walked slowly outside as if she was forcing them to their deaths.

"Where is your garden?" Laura asked as she rounded the corner of the house. The girls ran ahead, pointing to a weedy plot. "Let's see if we can find anything for the stew."

As long as she was near them, they managed to keep from fleeing back to the house, but they continued to cast fearful glances around. No vegetables had been planted and the garden had gone untended. However, she did find young onions from last year's planting. She gathered enough for the stew.

Noticing the barn reminded Laura to ask about their livestock.

"Well, the bear killed the milk cow one night and scared the horses so bad they ran away," answered Matthew.

When they returned to the cabin, she opened her bag of medicines to fix a strengthening tea for the mother.

By late afternoon, she had accomplished a number of tasks for the family. She had fed them and now had a stew simmering in the fireplace for their supper. Their mother had revived quicker than Laura had expected.

"You saved my family. How can I ever repay you?"

"Mrs. Wilson, I am so thankful I came when I did. I will be back tomorrow to check on you and the children. One thing I do want to ask you to do is not to allow your baby to nurse anymore. I think he drew poisons from your weakened body. He looks to be about two years old and can eat with the other children. He will be stronger for it. Will you do that?" Laura did not want her to lose what little strength she had gained. The mother nodded with relief on her face.

Laura mounted her mare and waved as she headed home. The day was gone, and it was getting dark. She was not as brave as she made out to be in front of the children about the gun and the bear. She became jumpier, seeing bear shapes materialize behind every tree as she made her way into her darkening valley. By the time she reached the cabin area, she was riding at full gallop as if a band of demons were after her.

Getting to the barn in half the time it usually took her, she unsaddled the horses, fed and watered them, closed up the chickens, and arrived at the cabin as the sun dropped below the western mountains, casting everything into total darkness.

CHAPTER 14

*L*aura returned to the Wilsons several more times during the next week. The family had grown stronger mentally and physically Mrs. Wilson cleaned herself, her children, and her home, expressing gratitude to Laura for all her help and concern. Matthew had gotten back his courage to begin hunting for the family again. On his first hunting trip away from the cabin, he found their horses in a meadow, grazing peacefully. He brought back a large turkey as well. Because of his newfound courage, he could provide for the family.

"Laura, I need to talk with you about an important matter. Will you come in and visit with me for a few minutes?" Mrs. Wilson asked as soon as Laura had ridden in. She sat Laura in front of the fireplace. "I have not asked about your husband and you have not mentioned him. Is something wrong?"

Laura, caught off guard by the question, did not respond right away. "He's had a difficult winter and is not well. He has not left the cabin for long periods. That's why he has not been able to help me with you and the children."

"Well, I did not want to be nosy, but I have a proposition I wanted to put to him about buying this place from me. I want to take the children and go back to our family in Georgia. I didn't want to come here, but my husband insisted. It hasn't been easy from the beginning, and it has gotten worse." Her voice broke.

Laura could not believe her ears. Now that she had money, she realized she could buy land all around her ranch. "We would be happy to buy this place from you, but are you sure you want to go back to Georgia? I have heard things back there are not the same since the war. So much has changed. If you are determined to go, what would you want for your place?" She looked around at the run down cabin.

"We bought 320 acres for fifty cents an acre. I would be happy to get half that much so we can get out of this hell hole," Mrs. Wilson answered vehemently.

"Let's make a deal. I need your help now. I need to go to Denver for a few days. If you will allow Matthew to care for my animals while I am gone, I will pay him twenty-five cents a day until I get back. I will pay you one dollar per acre for your land if you'll sign over the place to me no questions asked." She looked Mrs. Wilson in the eye. "Do you have the deed and the survey of the property?"

"Yes, I do, and my husband put the land in both of our names just in case something like this ever happened." She wiped tears from her cheeks with her apron. "Why do you want this place?"

"It's a hard land to survive in. I was terrified when I first came here and still am at times, but I can be myself here. I've learned to be strong in order to survive. I know I have to always be prepared for the unknown. I love this land, but it can be a cruel place as well. Will you sell me your land and let Matthew help me, too?"

After working out some details, they shook hands, and Laura took Matthew back with her to show him the trail and what she wanted him to do. She promised his mother he would return before dark.

Matthew came to the ranch the next day to teach Laura how to harness the team of horses. She would need the wagon when she took her gold to Denver. She planned to conceal the nuggets in fresh produce from her garden and pretend to be taking them to market. He agreed to come every day to check on the other livestock and feed the chickens until her return. He would gather the eggs to take home as well as any vegetables that matured.

Matthew said, "Your ranch looks like heaven compared to our place."

"It has been a backbreaking work to get this place to this point. Thank you."

After he had been there a little while, he asked, "Where is Mr. Brown?"

"I didn't want anyone to know, but I will tell you if you can keep my secret. He died several weeks ago. He had been sick and one day he keeled over. I didn't know what to do so I didn't tell anyone. I feel I can trust you to keep my secret. May I place my confidence in you?"

His chest swelled out and he said in his most manly voice, "You're special to me and my family, Miss Laura. I would die first before I told anyone."

She gave him her brightest smile. "I knew I could trust you. Now will you teach me which one of these damn traces goes where on this harness?" He began her lesson on how to harness a team. Laura was sure Matthew had his first crush because of the way he looked at her.

She practiced hitching the team to the wagon, then asked Matt to bring the wagon to the cabin and leave it so she could load what she wanted to take the next morning.

"I'll stay and help you."

"No, you have been a blessing to me today with all your help. It's getting late and you need to go home to your family. I will see you when I get back in five or six days."

"I should go with you to protect you," he pleaded.

"Thank you for your concern, but I truly need your help to take care of the place and you need to see after your family. Please don't fret. I'll have my guns with me. I will be very careful on the trail."

He reluctantly left, waving from the top of the ridge before disappearing.

Once he had gone, she began to haul the gold up from the cellar a bucket at a time. She made numerous trips up and down the steps before she got it all stowed into the wagon. She half-filled four baskets with gold nuggets and then placed early greens and vegetables on top.

Laura added a bedroll in case she could not make Denver by night-fall. Shivering at the idea of spending the night on the trail alone, she tried to prepare herself for any event. Rechecking her food items, bedding, cooking utensils, and clothes loaded into the wagon, she decided to dress as a man and braided her hair then tucked it under her hat. *I will smear a little soot on my face to give the appearance of an unkempt man.* Going to the fireplace, she selected a piece of charcoal and placed it on the table to remind her in the morning to use it.

Crawling into bed, she prayed a long prayer for the Wilsons, for forgiveness of all the lies she had told, and for a safe journey to and from Denver. She put all her trust in the Lord to keep her safe on the trail and to see her through.

~

Laura had been elated to see the sun rise shortly after she left home. As the light strengthened, so did the queasiness in the pit of her stomach. Pulling the team to a halt, she climbed down quickly and threw up the water she had drunk and some of last night's supper. She felt dizzy and ill. Holding onto the wagon wheel to keep from falling, the dizziness soon passed and she now felt hungry. It was crazy, but she was glad the illness had passed. She climbed back up on the wagon seat, retrieved her food basket, ate a biscuit, and drank more water. She probably should have eaten sooner. *Maybe not eating is what made me sick.* Feeling better, she urged the team toward Denver.

The day was long and tiring. She had forgotten how worn the road was and how the wagon bounced around in the deep ruts made by freight wagons. It had grown dark by the time she made it down the mountain, and the lights of Denver twinkled in the distance. *Oh, what a glorious sight!* She was almost there.

Laura felt relief as well as the tiredness from driving the team all day—a feat she had never imagined. Thoughts of a hot tub of water and a comfortable bed danced through her mind before the realization hit her she still had to make it to the bank. As she neared the edge of town, she saw other wagons pulling into town laden with supplies and produce. Urging her tired horses to go faster, she followed the others into town as a cover. Bright red, white, and blue banners waved from the storefronts. Posters nailed up on the buildings proclaimed the Fourth of July picnic, dance, and fireworks. A thrill ran through her exhausted body as she realized she would be in Denver for the exciting events. It had been way too long since she had enjoyed any kind of a celebration.

Stopping in front of the marshal's office, she spotted a young boy sitting on the steps. "Is the marshal in?"

"Naw, he went for supper at the hotel."

"Would you go get him and bring him back here? It's really important," she told him.

"It always is." He continued to sit there.

"If I gave you a dollar, would you go?" she asked.

"If you give it to me first, then I will go."

She fished a silver dollar out of her pocket, flashed it at him, and answered, "When you come back with the marshal, you get the dollar."

He jumped off the steps and raced away, yelling over his shoulder, "I'll bring him back. Don't go away!" Having money worked wonders.

She'd climbed down from the wagon to water her tired horses at a convenient trough, when the boy returned with the marshal in tow. "Here he is. Where is my dollar?" he demanded.

Laura thanked him for his help, handing him the shiny silver dollar. The marshal watched the exchange, but frowned as he turned, towering over her, "I am Marshal Joseph Roberts. What's so important you had to interrupt my supper?" he barked.

She could see in the lamplight he was a handsome man under the dusty hat. His face was clean-shaven, and he smelled of talc. If she was keeping score, cleanliness was in his favor.

"Yes, I need your help with something and I didn't know who to talk to or whom to trust. Have you been marshal here long?" she asked.

"What is your name? Who are you, and what do you want?"

She ignored his tone, "As I said before, I need someone I can trust with a special job. Are you that man or not?"

"I can be trusted to keep the law and protect the people. Is that what you want to know?"

"Glad to hear you can be trusted because I am in terrible need of someone who can keep his mouth shut. I don't want you to shoot anyone, so you needn't worry about that. I can explain better if you will agree to accompany me off the main street. What I want to show you is better seen in a less public place." She climbed up onto the wagon seat again and motioned for him to follow.

When he joined her, she whistled to the mares guiding them down the street. When she could turn into an alley and then behind the buildings, she stopped the team and turned to him. "First, Marshal Roberts, I am Laura Ralston. Yes, I know I am dressed in men's clothing but when you hear my story, you will understand why. I live up in the mountains and have come to Denver because I need help to get my gold to the bank without anyone being the wiser." Heart thudding, she rested her right hand on her gun in case she had chosen the wrong person.

He was quick to assure her he would help her. "What do you want me to do?"

"I need someone who can get the banker to come and open the back door so we can unload the gold, weigh it out, and deposit it in the bank. I have no one I can trust, so I reasoned out the marshal of Denver should be a good and trustworthy man, and I chose to take a chance. I will pay you for helping me. Will you bring the banker tonight before anyone knows what I have in my wagon?" she asked tiredly.

"You're smart, Laura Ralston. You've chosen the right man to help you. First, let's move the wagon on up the alley to the back of the bank. I saw the banker heading home not too long ago. I will fetch him. You need to stay here in the dark. Are you afraid?"

"Ace and I will wait right here for you and the banker," she whispered back to him.

"Ace? Who is Ace?" He looked around.

She patted the butt handle of her holstered six-shooter and said, "My pistol is my ace in the hole. You always have to have one."

He laughed softly as he jumped down from the wagon, "You have guts, Laura Ralston."

He soon returned without the banker. She was disappointed until she saw the back door of the bank open and a short fat man step out. Laura got down from the wagon to meet him, explained what she wanted them to do, and he agreed.

Marshal Roberts managed to carry each of the baskets into the bank as Laura watched. The long day's weariness settled in, and she yawned.

Mr. Little, the banker of Little & Little Bankers, put her gold in the vault. He wrote out a receipt for her and asked her to come back tomorrow when they would weigh the gold and finish their transaction.

Mr. Little asked, "Where are you staying?"

Laura looked from one man to the other and said, "I don't have a place to stay tonight. All I could think about was getting the gold here. As late as it is, I will stay with the horses and wagon in the livery until daylight."

Both men laughed at the idea. "As rich as you are, you could buy the hotel if they didn't have a room for you," Marshal Roberts said. "Come on, I'll take you over there."

"Thank you, but I need to care for the horses first, and get my things from the wagon," she said in protest.

"I'll send one of my deputies to take the wagon and horses to the livery stable while we get you settled in a room. He can bring your luggage to the hotel afterward. See you tomorrow, Mr. Little," he called over his shoulder as he took Laura's arm and guided her across the street to the nicest hotel in Denver and ordered her the best room in the place.

CHAPTER 15

*L*aura opened her eyes, wondering where she was. Heavy drapes prevented the light as well as noise from penetrating the room. Looking at the clock sitting on a nearby table, she could not believe it was eleven o'clock and she was still in bed. She jumped up, but was sorry she did because a wave of nausea swept over her. She made it to the chamber pot just in time to spew her guts.

A loud knock sent her scurrying for her robe. She opened the door to discover a large copper bathtub and two little Negro girls hiding behind it.

"Hello," she said. "Did you bring the tub up for me? I'm so glad you did. I need a bath to wash all of the trail dust off. Who is bringing the water?"

"We is," they chorused and giggled.

Opening the door wider to allow them to bring in the tub, she helped take it to the bathing room. When she'd come in last night, she had not noticed much about the room she had rented. She had barely managed to get in her gown and fall into bed. Now she could see how luxurious her accommodations were. She had a sitting room connected to the bedroom and bathing room. The furnishings were as nice as she had seen in Independence, but much newer. Her first thought was she could not afford this, but then she remembered she could. She laughed a loud.

"What are your names?" she asked the little girls. "And how old are you?"

"We is twins and we is nine years old. My name is Jasmine. I am the oldest by two minutes. This is my sister, Azalea. She is shy and doesn't talk much," related the less shy twin.

"It's nice to meet you both. My name is Laura, and I have a big favor to ask of you. I'll give each of you two bits if you will ask someone to please bring me a tray with breakfast. I'm starving. I haven't eaten since yesterday afternoon."

Before long, she had all the hot steamy water she needed and was soaking in the big tub. Lying back in the water, she remembered the people who had helped her to get to this point. She was so thankful to have gotten to Denver without any mishaps. As the water cooled, she began to lather the scented soap and bathe. She was excited to visit the banker for a final tally of her gold. She wanted to use the money wisely because it had come as a gift to her.

As she finished dressing in her work clothes and strapping her gun on her hip, another knock sounded on her door. "Missy Laura! I have your breakfast."

Laura opened the door wide to allow a tall, exotic black woman into the room with the heavy-laden tray of food. "My name is Sadie. I'm the cook here and the mother of the twins," she said proudly in her rich Cajun voice.

"I'm Laura. Thank you for bringing me food. I'm quite famished." Removing the plate covers, she surveyed eggs, bacon, hot biscuits, steak, mashed potatoes, and gravy, plus a large pot of coffee. "Oh, my. I only needed breakfast."

"Breakfast has long passed, and I didn't know what you might like to eat so I brought you some choices. Please enjoy whatever you like," Sadie wiped her hands on her flower-print apron and watched as Laura tasted everything she had brought.

"Oh my goodness! You are such a great cook," she exclaimed as she tried first one and then another dish. "I have another favor to ask of you. Will you arrange for a breakfast tray about seven o'clock every morning? And have the girls bring hot water about thirty minutes later? I will be happy to pay them. I have so much I need to do and so little time before I have to leave. I cannot sleep late again."

Sadie assured her, "I'll take care of everything. Thank you for your praise. I do love to hear if people like my cooking."

When Laura finished eating, she went over to the bank to find the banker. Mr. Little was delighted to see her again and escorted her into his office with great ceremony, as if she were a visiting queen.

"I've finished having your gold assayed and tallied. Here is the total in weight and dollars. Do you want to leave it here on deposit?" he asked hopefully.

Laura stared at the paper with the figures. "This…can't…be right."

"I have checked the figures myself," Mr. Little was quick to assure her.

"I never expected it to be such a large total. Can it be right?"

"I have my copy right here, and I will review it again to make sure it is all correct. If it is not, I will make the final adjustments for you," Mr. Little promised.

"You're a rich young woman. Are you married?" he asked.

Laura looked up from the paper, making direct eye contact with him. "You are my banker, Mr. Little. Therefore, I would appreciate the courtesy you afford other customers of not asking any personal questions. If the time ever presents itself where I want to tell anyone about my life, you will be the first to know. Is that understood?"

"Yes, Miss Laura. I understand I was out of line asking such a personal question."

"This is not illegal gain. I didn't steal it from anyone. It is a gift from God. However, I would appreciate it if neither you nor any of your employees discuss my business or me with anyone. If I find out you have, I will take my business elsewhere. Are we in agreement?"

"Your business is your affair. Anything we talk about will be kept in strict confidence."

"Now then, I want the account in the name of Laura Ralston. Get me the papers I need to sign to deposit this in your bank and I want five hundred dollars now. After we have that taken care of, I have some private business I want you to help me with. Before I leave town, I will give you a letter for the marshal. I appreciate all he has done to help me and I want to reward him. I would like you to deliver it for me, but only after I leave. Will you take care of it for me?"

"Happy to help you in any way I can," he said.

"I am buying property adjoining my ranch. I am not sure how often I will get back to Denver, so if I send you a letter is it possible for money to be transferred from bank to bank?" She forced herself to get over the shock of her sudden wealth and get down to business.

She left the bank and headed to the livery stable to check on her horses and the vegetables still in the wagon. She hoped to arrange with the general store owner to buy the fresh produce. The horses were well cared for, but the owner of the livery stable told her he couldn't believe she had made it to Denver with a cracked tongue and an axle that was almost in pieces. "Yes, little gal, the Lord was taking care of you last night. You could have broken down at any point. This wagon has seen some hard use. What have you been hauling, rocks?" He spit a long, brown stream of tobacco juice onto the stable floor. Her stomach did a flip-flop, and she almost lost her breakfast.

"Do you have another wagon I could buy?" she asked.

"What type do you want? I have a fancy surrey or a smaller work wagon pulled by a two-horse team or a newer one like what you got here, but a four-horse team pulls it. Do you have a husband? He should decide which one he needs."

She stood there trying to decide how best to answer his question. "I'll be back later to discuss purchasing a wagon. Thank you for helping me."

As she turned to leave, Marshal Roberts came through the livery door and grinned at her.

"I was looking for you," Laura said. "I have another problem and I'll need your help again." The man looked even better in daylight.

"Joseph Roberts, at your service, Lady in Distress," He took his hat off and bowed to her. She grinned at his antics.

"My wagon is busted and I'll have to purchase a new one before I can go home, but I need help from someone with a little more knowledge about such things. Also, I had planned to buy some brood mares. I want to raise horses on my ranch. I relate better to horses than cattle."

Several hours later, with Joseph's help, she had bought a new steadier wagon pulled by a team of four horses. She was told it had a smoother ride and was easier on the horses to have the extra two to help pull the weight. Instead of the two brood mares, Joseph had helped her pick four mares out of good sturdy stock.

Joseph asked her what kind of stud she had and she blinked at him. "Well, how will you raise horses if you don't have a stud to service them?" He chuckled.

"This is a new plan. I am trying to grow my ranch. Please don't make fun of me, sir," she replied heatedly. He chuckled at her as he helped carry the vegetables to the general store where she left a list of supplies.

She needed new clothes suitable for Denver and work clothes for her return to the ranch but was unfamiliar with the town. Joseph directed her to a French dressmaker down the block. He walked with her to the little shop.

"Will you have dinner with me tonight at seven? I get my dinner break about then. I could meet you downstairs in your hotel, and we could eat there."

"I'm not sure if I will have anything appropriate to wear. All I have to wear are these men's clothes, but perhaps I will find some dresses. All right! I will see you at seven."

Later in the afternoon, she left the dress shop laden with packages of underclothes, women's shoes, bonnets, and three beautiful dresses, the likes of which she had never seen before. She hurried to her room to clean up and put on one of the lovely gowns. But which one?

Laura stared transfixed at the image in the floor length cheval mirror. *Who is this? Can this be me?* The green and white stripes of the damask cloth accented her fair skin and fit her slim frame to perfection. She had braided her blonde hair, wrapping the braids around her head to create the appearance of a halo in the lamplight.

Sometime after seven o'clock, she descended the stairs to find Joseph waiting in the lobby. Even as inexperienced as she was with men, she saw approval in his eyes. And something else she was not sure about.

"I am so sorry to keep you waiting, Joseph." As he took her hand and kissed it, her cheeks heated.

"My pleasure. It was worth the wait for you to come down. You are lovely tonight. I can't help but compare the dirty faced boy/girl—I wasn't sure which—that I met last night, to this beautiful image before me," he finished huskily, continuing to hold her hand.

"These are for you." He presented her with a bouquet of red roses.

"Oh, Joseph, they're beautiful." She sniffed the sweet perfume of the roses as she fought back tears that threatened to spill forth.

"What is wrong, Laura?"

"No one has ever given me flowers before, and I'm touched by your thoughtfulness. They are my favorite. Thank you."

Still holding her hand, he led her to a private table covered with a white cloth in the corner of the dining room. When they ordered their meal, the waitress asked Laura if she could put the flowers in water for her. She returned with them in a vase of water and set them in the middle of the table making a wonderful centerpiece for their dining.

After dinner, while they were enjoying pie and coffee, Joseph asked Laura where she came from. She told him about her family in Independence and about growing up in a big city.

"But how did you get out here?"

She stared at him for a few moments before she said, "My parents had dear friends who ran a private school which my siblings and I attended. I was the oldest daughter and loved going to school. I read everything I could find. When I was fifteen, my father, who was the yard boss at a big sawmill, was injured. Our family didn't know how we were going to survive. One day, my father announced he would receive a stipend from the sawmill, if I married the owner. I was forced into an unwanted marriage to help my family.

"One day my husband announced we were moving out West. He sold his sawmill and wanted to find adventure. Of course, he hadn't said anything to me. It was the saddest day in my life when I had to say goodbye to my family. I didn't know if we would ever see each other again. When we got to Denver, he bought land high in the rugged mountains. By the grace of God, we have survived. I know it's not commonplace to see a woman in pants, but I've learned a lot about how to survive. I can see you have lots of questions by the look on your face."

"Where is your husband now? Why are you here alone?"

"I knew that would be your first question. He's been ill, so I was the only one strong enough to bring the gold to Denver. I haven't told anyone my business except you, and I felt it was right you know because you've been the one person here I have depended on to help me make important decisions. Will you keep my confidences?"

"I'm disappointed to find out you're married. I had hoped we could become better acquainted before you left. You are a smart and desirable woman, Laura. I know how hard the winters can be in the mountains. Many people have died trying to survive up there. You are smart and tough. I saw that from the beginning and you will survive." He placed his hand over hers on the table.

"You've been so wonderful to help me, and I didn't want you to continue to think I was available. I would like to become friends, if a man and woman can be." She watched his brown eyes glowing warmly back at her.

When they finished their dessert, he escorted her up the three flights of stairs to the top of the hotel where her suite was located. She unlocked the door and turned to say goodnight to him. He pulled her into his arms and whispered, "I know you're married, but please kiss me goodnight to make it a perfect evening for me."

She allowed him to kiss her, liking the feel of his lips on hers as she placed her arms around his waist and hugged him to her warming body. Her curves fit perfectly into his body as her desires began to rise. She could feel his arousal grow as the kiss deepened. He moaned with pleasure when she opened her mouth to his searching tongue.

"Honey, I like it when you open for me," he whispered into her hair.

Her desire grew as well. Her breathing increased keeping pace with his. Although she was tempted to invite him in to see what would happen next, reality overcame her sexual desire for this man and she released his body.

They stepped back from each other. "I knew you were full of fire," he said. "I wish you would burn me to a crisp."

"I like the way you kiss. Maybe someday I'll be free to find out more about you. Good night, Joseph," she whispered then tenderly touched his lips with hers.

When she closed the door on the biggest temptation she had ever faced, she was on fire and desired him. She began to realize she had desires and needs to be satisfied, and they could consume her. She would have to be more careful next time or they both would go up in flames.

CHAPTER 16

*L*aura was dressed and coming down the back stairs before seven o'clock the next morning, even though it had been late before she settled down and gone to bed. She had played with her new clothes, trying them on and whirling in front of the mirror to see how she looked. She chuckled to herself because she had never had a problem like this before.

Last night, after she'd settled down, she had written letters to her family back in Independence so she could post them before she left. She did not tell them anything about her gold or about Abner's death. She described things to them to let them know she was happy and doing well. She had never told them about how her life truly was because then they would worry and fret over her. It was late before she turned out her lamp and went to bed.

She descended the stairs in the morning pleased because she had not had any of the stomach upsets she had been experiencing since coming to Denver. But as she reached the bottom near the kitchen, her senses were overwhelmed with the smells of cooking. She ran for the back door and out into the alley before throwing up with gusto. Laura leaned against the building wall until she could regain her composure. Why did this happen when she smelled food? Still puzzled, she walked over to the well, drew up a fresh bucket of water, and washed her face, rinsing her mouth out before going back inside.

Sadie and the twins greeted her happily. "Why are you in here?" Sadie asked. "We'll serve you breakfast out in the dining room." She tried to usher her in there.

"I'd like to have breakfast with you and the girls, if it's all right? I don't want to sit alone. It will be much more fun in here," she said winking at the twins.

"All right you can sit in here, but no giggling," Sadie said to Laura who started to giggle setting the twins off.

As Sadie set a plate of food before her, a large black man appeared in the doorway. "Who's this?" he demanded.

Sadie led him over to the table. "This is my husband, John Long."

Laura extended her hand in greeting.

Hesitantly, John shook it.

Sadie set his breakfast before him and asked Laura, "What have you gotten done since we last talked?"

"I purchased a newer and larger wagon because the other was busted, and I had to buy four new horses to pull the larger wagon."

John snorted loudly, unable to contain himself.

Female eyes turned in his direction as his wife said in a no-nonsense tone, "And what is so funny?"

"Well, first I find it funny this pretty white lady is sitting in the kitchen eating with black folk. Second, she now has a four up team to pull her new wagon. Do you even know how to drive a four-up team and wagon?" he asked her.

"I …I…uh…drove the wagon with two horses to Denver. I guess it will be the same but with four horses going back."

Her answer caused him to explode in loud guffaws, "Ma'am, if you plan to get home anytime soon, you need driving lessons or you and them new horses will not get out of town."

"I'll pay you to teach me," she told him because she had already had the same concerns he voiced.

"How much?"

Laura quoted a price, and he took it. "When can you start?" Laura asked before he could back out.

"I have chores at the hotel and will be done at nine o'clock," he answered.

"Great! I need to go to the general store to check on my supplies and if you will pick up the wagon and horses at the livery stable we'll go have some driving lessons. I'll wait for you there," she told John as she hurried from the kitchen.

The general store was booming with business early this morning. Laura had been able to shop in peace without the shopkeeper trying to sell her things she did not need or want. In the past, she had not been able to think about such things but now she could. The readymade shirts and pants were too large for her, but she wondered if the French seamstress could alter them for her before she had to leave. She needed a new pair of boots as well. She hoped he had a pair that would fit her.

Overhearing one of the customer's request for his general delivery mail from the young boy behind the counter reminded Laura she had forgotten to call for her mail when she arrived. How could she have been so stupid? She had given her friends on the wagon train this address when they left and Abner had posted some letters to others back home. When the customer had moved on, Laura stepped up and asked if he would check to see if she had any mail. He asked her name and she said Laura Brown. He checked through several stacks in the B slot and came up with two letters addressed to her. He said he had another one addressed to Abner Brown. She replied, "He's my brother who is at the livery stable. I'll take it to him." The young boy gave her the letter without hesitation. She wanted to rip them open but fought her temptation to do so. Placing them in her purse with her money, she continued to shop for work clothes, various tools she needed, and cloth to make aprons, dish towels, and other linens that had worn thin.

The storekeeper came over to ask her about some of the items on the list she had given him. She added the items she'd found and asked him to keep a running tab and stack the items separately from everyone else's order. She would pay him cash when she picked up the supplies. He also found young boys' boots that were her size. Thrilled for the first time to have boots that fit her, she added them to her stash. She decided on two pairs of pants and two shirts in boys' sizes to take to the dressmaker. He put them on her tab. She arranged with him to pick up the supplies the night before she planned to leave. She would have her wagon at the back of his store and provide help to load it. Pleased to be paid in cash, he was very accommodating.

John waited in front with the team and wagon until she left the dress-maker's shop. She climbed up on the wagon seat to sit beside him as he clucked to the team, slapping them with the reins.

John and Laura went a little way out of town before he stopped the team and offered her the reins. "Now we begin."

Several hours later, a tired and sore Laura, an exhausted John, and a confused team of horses returned to the livery stable. Laura began to walk to the hotel, but John insisted she wait until he could follow her to make sure she was safe. He reminded her outlaws frequented the saloons watch-ing for easy prey like herself. She knew he was right, so she agreed to wait for him since she had forgotten her gun.

On the way back to the hotel, they stopped off again at the general store for Laura to buy a small derringer she could conceal in her purse. At the same time, she had the shopkeeper add to her list a number of pistols and five rifles complete with ammunition.

As they left the store, John remarked, "You're the most unusual female I have ever met. Are you afraid of anything?"

"Oh John, I stay in a normal state of fear. But I've taught myself to shoot so I am able to protect myself and my property from whatever may come."

When they arrived at the hotel, Laura thanked John for all his help as she hurried upstairs. Anxious to get to her room where she could read the letters burning a hole in her purse, she opened the envelope addressed to Abner first. Dated two years prior, it was from his attorney. After she read it, she began to cry. It stated the sale of his family home had been completed and the funds were waiting for him to send instructions for disbursement. He had never told her anything about his business. He could have had the money wired to him at any time. She sat thinking of the "what ifs." Such a large amount would have paid off the ranch and left them with a comfortable nest egg. But she did not want anything to do with his money. Later, she would see his children got it, but not now. She was more concerned about how to secure the ranch legally for herself. In reading the letter from the attorney, she was concerned his children could claim her ranch. She needed to do something to prevent it. But what? She had seen an attorney's office next to the doctor's sign. She had contemplated visiting the doctor to find out what kind of stomach ailment she had because her teas were not helping her. Forgetting her other letters, she hurried down the stairs and headed toward the lawyer's door.

Laura knocked on the door below the sign proclaiming, *George Miller, Attorney at Law.* At a distant "come in," she opened the door. She was not prepared to see a shirtless man with shaving cream all over his face. He almost cut his throat as he brought his razor up in a crooked fashion. "Oh, excuse me for interrupting you," as she quickly turned around.

"Let me finish up and I will be right with you." Wiping shaving cream from his face he went into the back room, closing the door behind him.

When he returned, he was dressed and clean-shaven. "My name is George Miller. How may I help you?" He offered her a chair and motioned for her to sit down.

"I am Laura Ralston Brown. I am in need of a lawyer who can help me with a delicate matter. It has to do with land my husband bought in his name. What will happen to me and our land, if he dies?"

"Does he have a will? Or a letter stating you would be the owner if anything happened to him?" he questioned.

"No, I do not think so," she said. "I found a couple of gold nuggets and used them to pay off a loan on the land and supplies he had gotten on credit. I have a receipt in my name."

"Where was the land purchased and the deed recorded?"

"When we were here in Denver, he bought it sight unseen from a miner. It is recorded here. Is there any way I can change it into my name?"

"Mrs. Brown, is your husband dead?"

"Do I have your assurance that what we talk about is confidential?"

"Absolutely. If he has already passed, we can file to have the papers changed into your name as his beneficiary. Do you have any children?" he asked.

"No, but he has grown children back in Missouri where we used to live, and I am concerned they might try to take my ranch," she said.

She opened the oilcloth-wrapped packet of letters she had brought with her. "I have papers stating I paid off the loan on the ranch with my money and a final letter he left because he knew he was dying, but he never told me he was ill. It happened very suddenly. Will this help?" she asked.

"Okay, tell me everything you can or know about your husband, were you forced to marry, or if you were forced to come here and what you know about his children. Leave nothing out. I think I can help you, but it will cost to get it done. Do you understand?"

Several hours later, she left the office, pleased with how their meeting had gone. He was sure he could help, and she was grateful. Her plans were coming together to secure the ranch for herself. She had left the attorney with a nice retainer and the promise of more if he could help her.

She paused at the doctor's door and started to go in but could not bring herself to because she felt fine. What could she tell the doctor? She felt great and threw up when she smelled food. How ridiculous! She went on to her hotel and up to her room where she began to read the two letters from her mother and another from her sister, Jane.

CHAPTER 17

Sadie brought up Laura's breakfast early the next morning. She would eat breakfast, and then the twins would bring hot water for a bath. Laura was anxious to go home, but saddened to leave her new-found friends.

When Laura lifted the cover off the food, she bolted for the chamber pot. Sadie rushed around, getting her a wet cloth for her head and helping her back to a chair to rest. When she had recovered, she thanked Sadie and added, "I don't know what is wrong with me. I throw up every time I see or smell food."

"How long have you been having this ailment?"

"Oh, it started about the time I headed here," she said, a little stronger now she had begun to recover. "I have been drinking some of my healing teas but nothing seems to help and it comes on suddenly—like now when I'm not expecting it to happen."

Sadie threw a knowing look at Laura, but did not say anymore on the subject. "Hope you'll feel like eating soon. The twins will be up soon with hot water for your bath. They love helping you, so you shoo them back down when you're done. I have work for them to do today," she added as she headed for the door.

Sadie closed the door, allowing Laura her privacy before the twins arrived. Laura had coins ready for them and as they finished the tiring chore of hauling buckets of hot water three flights up, she placed two quarters in each of their palms. They were delighted by the extra money and hurried out to show their mother.

Shortly after the twins left, a knock sounded on Laura's door. George Miller, the attorney, asked for a few minutes of her time. Surprised by his visit, she invited him into the parlor.

"I have just returned from recording the deed papers in your name at the courthouse. Judge Hastings agreed with me that Abner's final letter granted title to you. Because you were successful in paying it off, you have preserved it for yourself and your future heirs. You will be able to return home secure knowing it's yours."

Laura began to weep then regained her composure. "Since I'll not be returning to Denver for a while, will you continue to work as my lawyer? I will send letters of requests for any needs I might have in the future. I'm purchasing the adjoining ranch. Will you see it gets properly recorded when I send you the papers?"

"I'll be happy to do whatever is needed to help you in the future," he answered as he took his leave.

~

Marshal Roberts invited Laura on a picnic. She was excited about having such a handsome escort to show her the area around Denver.

Around noon, Joseph knocked on her door. Laura greeted him warmly as he pulled her into his arms kissing her. She enjoyed the kiss and kissed him back. Before it got out of hand, Laura stepped back. "We must be going now."

With a sigh, Joseph released her, "I wanted a morning kiss to see if the fire is still there, and it is." He opened the door for her to precede him.

When they met Sadie in the lobby to retrieve the picnic basket she had prepared for them, Laura blushed when she saw Sadie looking closely at her, and Joseph was grinning happily.

Joseph helped Laura into the buggy and then settled by her side. He grabbed the reins and clucked to the horse to giddy up. He had the perfect place picked out for their picnic. The day was warm although a light cool breeze was blowing down from the mountains.

Laura had chosen to wear one of her new dresses today with its low-cut neckline exposing the tops of her breasts. The heavy wool shawl around her shoulders slipped off from the constant motion of the buggy exposing her to his sensual perusal.

They traveled for a while, enjoying the beautiful day, before he turned off the main road heading in the direction of a stream near a grove of trees in the distance.

Jumping down to tie the horse, Joseph came around to help Laura down. She wandered over to the edge of the stream to watch the trout lazily swimming by. "I wish I had brought my fishing pole," he said.

"I like to fish," she said. "When I get tired of deer meat, I go and catch a bunch of trout. Some I fry, and the rest I smoke to save for winter."

"You have learned to live off the land, haven't you?"

"I will never forget the first winter we were there. We almost ran out of food because we didn't prepare for such a harsh winter. I have learned to preserve food from a garden as well as smoke meat or can it for the long winters. There were times we couldn't leave our cabin because the snow reached to the roofline. It's terrifying knowing you can't get out."

"I know it was terrifying for you. But I can tell from what you have said you have grown stronger from your experiences. You have grown from a girl to a beautiful and strong woman." He took her in his arms to comfort her.

Laura enjoyed his encouraging words and his protective arms. He leaned down, capturing her lips with his. The contact with his body excited and thrilled her, but Laura had begun to recognize the danger signs. She soon tried to step back from him.

"You don't need to fear me," he told her with a ragged breath. "I would never hurt you, but you do know I desire you."

"I think this picnic was a mistake. I shouldn't have agreed to come alone with you since I'm a married woman." She moved farther away from him.

"Let's enjoy the food Sadie prepared for us, and then we will go back to town." He retrieved the basket and blanket from the buggy and began to spread it out.

Laura hesitated for a moment before allowing Joseph to help her sit down on the blanket. As they were eating, she asked about his life, hoping to move the subject away from their relationship—or lack thereof.

They spent several hours eating and talking about their families. While they ate and talked, Laura felt as if they were being watched. Glancing around, she saw nothing to be alarmed with, so continued her picnic with Joseph. Before long, it was time to drive back to town. Joseph helped her pick up the plates, food, and blanket and stowed them in the buggy. Taking her arm, he assisted her into the buggy.

When they returned to town, they stopped at the hotel to get John and Laura's new wagon. John followed them to the back of the general store. The men could not believe the amount of supplies Laura purchased and commented about it.

"I don't know when I'll be able to come back and visit," she explained. When it was loaded, they tied a tarp over the wagon bed so none of her precious cargo would get wet if it rained. And it always rained in the mountains.

When Laura got back to the hotel, the twins were waiting to show her their mother's herb garden in planters on their back porch. Laura glanced at Sadie when she recognized some of the same plants she had been taught to use. "Are you a healer, Sadie?" Laura asked.

Smiling happily at the question Sadie said, "It's a family thing. I am not as good as my sister, Martha, but I do have knowledge about healing and other things. Are you a healer as well?"

"Well, I guess you could say I have some knowledge about herbs and special healing teas, but I haven't healed anyone. However, I've wanted to learn more because when you live in the mountains doctors are too far away. I met a wonderful person on the wagon train who taught me about the healing effects of herbs and barks from certain trees. I learned more from an Indian girl whose mother is a medicine woman when we settled on our ranch. She taught me about the kinds of herbs growing here and their healing effects."

"I met the Indian maiden quite by chance one day when I shot a bear to keep it from attacking her," she related the story to them as awe lit up their faces. They insisted on knowing more.

"The bear was attacking her, when I shot it with my rifle. Well, uh… actually, I shot off half his left ear. Then he ran away. We became fast friends after that happened."

The twins shouted with glee at her story of the bear and the Indian girl.

Sadie watched Laura with a growing interest as she talked to the twins. "Laura, are you aware you have a strong aura around you? I sense there is much more to you and your story."

"I seem to be able to draw animals to me. I am able to sense their needs and help them."

"I sensed that about you. I saw visions of you before you came. Does that frighten you? I know you're on a journey and as you learn you're becoming stronger. You said you met a woman who taught you about healing. I am praying it might have been my sister, Martha," she whispered as she held her breath.

"The woman I met was named Amanda. She and her husband were going on to California," answered Laura.

"Oh. Martha was big and tall like our father. She was a healer and a wonderful cook as well. We were separated when we were younger because she was sold to a man in New Orleans who kept her for a while before the war started. Somehow, she secured her freedom. I found out later she came West either by wagon train or on her own. She had strength in body and spirit to survive. She also had special abilities. I need to find her. There have been many times I knew she was alone and afraid," Sadie wept quietly.

"I'm sorry it wasn't your sister." Laura held Sadie in her arms and allowed her to cry. "Perhaps someday you'll find her. I've wanted to ask if you and John would consider working for me at my ranch in the mountains. It is rough and rugged, but it's beautiful. Next spring, I'll build several cabins and I would like for you, John, and the twins to come work for me.

John can work the ranch and horses and you can help me cook and garden. Talk to John and see if he is agreeable to working for a woman. Can either of you read?"

Sadie wiped her tears. "When we were slaves, we were forbidden to learn to read and write by the masters, but there were those who knew the war was coming and secretly taught any who wanted to learn. I wanted to learn to read and write badly. And I did."

"I'll need people who can read and write. I am planning to build my ranch by raising horses. Will you and John come work for me?"

"Miss Laura, I would love it. I'll talk to John tonight, and he'll give you our answer in the morning. You are a blessed person with a mission in this life. Your journey won't be easy, but it will be one made just for you and all the people around you."

"Thank you, Sadie. I sense you have powers, although I am unsure what they are. I know I need you to be with me at the ranch."

~

Sadie prepared a celebration meal to say farewell to Laura. Everyone tried to be happy, but there was sadness in seeing Laura go. The twins liked their new friend and cried when they had to say goodbye. John and Sadie took their two tired little girls to their sleeping quarters. Laura's wagon was parked in the alley between the hotel and their quarters so John could keep watch over it during the night. Joseph would check on him to make sure all was well.

Laura planned to leave before daybreak the next morning with John and Joseph escorting her across the plains until she reached the base of the mountains. The two men were not happy about her plans. Too many things could happen to a woman alone on the trail, but she insisted she had gotten to Denver alone, and she would find her way home alone. She was an amazingly courageous and determined woman.

Joseph followed Laura up the stairs to her hotel room door. When she opened it, she turned to thank him for a wonderful day. As she did so, he pulled her into his arms, kissing her passionately. "Please let me come in and spend the night with you, sweetheart." He kissed his way down her neck to the exposed flesh above her breasts. She sucked in her breath as she arched her back, enjoying the pleasant sensations she had been missing— sweet temptations to let him come in. *Who would know? Who would care?* Then in the next breath, *I would.* She could not lead Joseph into thinking of them as a couple. She had to tell him they could not be together. She knew she was attractive to him and felt herself weakening. Thoughts of what the night would hold if she let him come in circled in her head. A sudden loud noise at the bottom of the stairs brought them both back to earth.

Wanting to hurry Joseph along, Sadie shouted back down the stairs as if John was waiting for her, "I'll be down after I've helped Laura with her packing. Now you go on and see to the twins." She stomped up the stairs.

Looking up as Joseph and Laura looked downward at her, she said, "Why Joseph, I thought you had already said your good night. Sorry to interrupt, but I needed to help Laura with her packing," she continued up to Laura's door.

Joseph looked sadly at Laura, kissing her on the cheek, "Good night and sweet dreams. I'll see you early in the morning." In frustration, he stomped down the front stairs.

Laura turned to Sadie saying, "What are you up to?"

"I have a special gift for you, Miss Laura. I know why you've been ill since you came. You are going to have a baby."

Her words hurt. "No, Sadie, it's not possible. I'm barren and unable to have children."

"I'm not sure who convinced you that you are barren, but you're with child. You may not want to admit who the father is, but whether it is your dead husband's or not, you are going to have a baby," Sadie replied to her with tenderness and understanding.

"How did you know my husband was dead?" she whispered.

"Another of my family secrets. I am a dreamer of dreams, and seer of visions. I see things to come, and I see things about people's pasts or their futures. Sometimes, when it happens, I don't know what it means, but it usually comes true. I know your dead husband is not the one who has made you so happy. There were others since his death, and now they, too, are gone, but the babe will be a blessing for you in the future. I know you will be happy in your heart, but I also know Marshal Roberts will not cause it. He's not the man for you. You must forget him. His destiny does not lie with yours. I'm not telling you these things to frighten you, but to let you know you'll be fine and someday happy with your life." She hugged Laura tightly.

"The woman on the wagon train told me she could read palms. She said I would have children someday, but I didn't believe her since Abner convinced me I was barren. Now you tell me I'm with child and I know it could not be from my dead husband. Although, I will tell everyone it is his to protect my child from ridicule, because I will never marry again. I was forced to once, but never again," she told Sadie.

"Sadie, if you can see the past and my future, why can't you locate or find your sister?"

"This gift I have cannot be controlled. I see visions, but I can only tell a person what it shows. Most times, it is bits and pieces until the time of fulfillment. I've been shown events in your life and know we are connected somehow in the future. When you asked me to come to the ranch, another piece fell into place. After our first meeting, I saw a beautiful place with a stream of water flowing down through a meadow. Is it your ranch?"

"Oh my gosh, Sadie! It sounds like it is the place on my ranch near where I plan to build cabins for people who work for me." She hugged Sadie again. "Do you have any idea how we are connected except by being good friends?"

"No, it hasn't been revealed to me. The only vision I've seen is you with more children and your gifts passing to them as well." She happily relayed this news to a surprised Laura.

"My children. What wonderful news to someone who believed she was barren."

They talked and packed Laura's belongings.

After they finished, Laura hugged Sadie again. "Someday I may tell you how my baby came into being. However, for now it will remain my secret. Sadie nodded knowingly.

Sadie left and Laura lay down on the bed, dressed in her comfortable pants and shirt, ready to hit the trail when the time came. As soon as John woke her, she would pull on her boots and grab her hat. However, sleep did not come quickly. So many thoughts and memories swirled through her mind as she placed her hand on her stomach thinking again of the two angel men who had come and gone during her journey. Settling her thoughts down, she slept.

It seemed like a short time before John knocked on the door. Time to go. He helped her load her things into the wagon, including a large dinner basket from Sadie, as they waited for Joseph to appear.

CHAPTER 18

The full moon had risen sometime after midnight flooding the trail with bright light leading across the valley from Denver to the base of the mountains where Laura's escorts would turn back. They had made better time than she had on her journey toward Denver in the ramshackle wagon. And before long, the sun would be coming up. She could see the faint glow in the east.

Laura climbed down from the seat where she had placed a thick quilt to sit on, trying to make the ride a little more comfortable. "I don't know how to repay either of you for all your help. I value your friendship very much." She hugged each man and wiped tears from her cheeks.

John said, "Thank you, Missy Laura, for your kind offer of a job for me and Sadie. We're happy to accept it."

"I am so pleased you'll come to the ranch and work for me, John."

Joseph released her and she stepped back to gaze up at him. "You have been a true gentleman. Thank you is not enough."

She followed them around, watching while they checked and double-checked the wagon and team making sure all was right. Besides the four new mares pulling the heavy vehicle, her other two mares were tied to the back.

As the sun began to peek over the mountains spreading its warm glow, they knew the time had come to say their final good-byes. John said, "God bless and keep you safe and happy, Missy Laura!" She nodded as she wiped tears of sadness and joy from her eyes.

Joseph stepped up, encircling her with his arms again. It felt good to feel safe for a few moments. "Please come back to me, Laura. I need you," he whispered as he kissed her lips one last time, and then he helped her to get on the wagon.

She grabbed the reins, released the wagon brake, and whistled to the team. "Ladies, let's go home." She could not bring herself to glance back at the men because tears were burning her eyes. She would go forward to whatever God had in store for her whether it was good or bad. She knew He would see her though.

The trail became clearer as the sun rose higher over the mountain. As she headed up the rough road, it became narrower with the trees and brush growing closer to the wagon ruts. It was no smoother on the way up than it had been on the way down. The weight of the heavier wagon helped as it bounced along. But not much. The trail was still rough, no matter what. As she approached a small clearing, a large screaming eagle with its talons extended swooped down from the sky startling her.

Sensing the bird of prey was offering a warning, she became more alert to her surroundings. As she rounded the next bend with high boulders on either side, she saw it was a perfect place for an ambush. Suddenly, a tough-looking man holding a gun stepped out from one of the boulders, waving for her to stop. Recognizing him as one of the men who worked for Tuffy, and who had followed her, she knew he wanted to hurt her or take her back to Tuffy. She urged the team to a faster pace with no intention of stopping as he raised his gun to shoot one of the lead horses. She did not wait to find out his intentions, but instead drew her pistol, shooting his gun hand before he could fire.

A flash of sunlight on a rifle barrel in the boulders drew her attention, and she fired at the gun pointed in her direction. Whether it was expert shooting or dumb luck, her hot lead found the gunpowder in the rifle barrel causing it to explode in the outlaw's face. She heard a loud explosion and a scream as she continued at breakneck speed up the mountain.

The wagon sped by the gunman lying next to the road, holding his hand with a bullet hole through it and cussing her for the she-devil he knew her to be.

Laura was frightened by the ambush; she pushed the horses hard, racing around dangerous curves. As she began to calm down, she slowed the horses as well, talking to them in soothing tones. Easing them into a comfortable pace, she soon found a place near a spring to stop and rest them.

Glancing around to make sure she was not followed, she secured the reins, set the brake and climbed down taking her rifle with her. Her six-shooter strapped to her leg and hip gave her comfort, but if she encountered a bear, she would need the power of a rifle. Getting several wooden buckets from the wagon, she headed in the direction of running water.

After she gave each horse a drink to cool them down, she talked softly to each one, petting and scratching their ears. She thanked them for working hard to take her out of harm's way. Climbing up on the wagon seat, she picked up the reins, saying, "Ladies, nice and easy now!"

By noon, they were almost home. It amazed her the way four horses could eat up miles. She remembered the hard journey down the mountain with the gold and two horses. She felt ashamed now, knowing what a strain she had put on those two. She had learned so much from John about the horses sharing the weight of pulling the wagon. She was happy her first two mares were tied to the back, and not pulling the wagon.

Deciding to take a break, Laura searched for a place where she could pull off the narrow trail in case another wagon or riders came along. Finding a wide spot to stop, she eased the mares into a shaded area with a rushing stream nearby. Tying them securely, she hauled water to the mares again.

Laura prepared six feedbags with oats for them because they had not eaten since last night. They needed food and rest and so did she. After attaching the feedbags to each horse, she grabbed her rifle and her dinner basket and went to sit under a tall pine tree. Sadie had filled the basket with all her favorite foods—fried chicken, fresh vegetables, sourdough bread and best of all, slices of apple pie. After eating, she became drowsy. As she eased back against the tree, the long weary hours and the short night took their toll on her.

She did not know how long she slept, but as she woke, something furry was lying next her. She slowly opened her eyes to see Silver. He had been guarding her and waiting for her to wake up. "Oh, Silver!" she cried, hugging him close, feeling his soft, beautiful fur, and gazing at his piercing blue eyes. She did not know how he always knew where to find her, but he did. Did he sense her? She felt better knowing he was here.

The mares did not like the wolf around them and were becoming nervous. However, she talked to each one of them, explaining the wolf would not harm them. They seemed to understand. Gathering up the feedbags, she watered each horse again before continuing the rest of the journey. Laura felt refreshed and sensed the horses did too. Silver followed behind.

Mid afternoon, she approached the trail to her ranch. The logs and limbs were still arranged the way she had placed them when she left. She had asked Matthew to come through the woods but never the same way twice. She did not want paths that could be followed to her cabin. After the attack on the road, she knew Tuffy was still looking for her. She did not want anyone to find her easily. Moving the logs aside, she made enough room for the horses and wagon to pass through. Replacing everything, she picked up a branch using it like a broom to erase the horses' hoof marks and wagon tracks and moved loose leaves over everything. Anyone who approached the cabin would be someone who already knew where to find her. And there were few people who knew.

She decided she would wait for Matthew to come tomorrow to unload. After backing the wagon to the front porch, and setting the brake, she placed rocks in front and back of the wheels to prevent it from rounding. Unhitching the horses, she led them to the barn to remove the harnesses and she turned them out into the hidden valley. They ran, jumped, and kicked up their heels glad to be free of the leather and chains. Before long, they settled down and began to eat the luscious green grass.

The penned chickens made squawking noises at her when she scattered grain in their pen. She laughed at their fussing, promising them tomorrow they would be free to roam and scratch wherever they wanted.

She was anxious to unload her new clothes and other personal things she had bought. As she removed the tarp at the back of the wagon, she sucked in her breath. A beautiful oak cradle on rockers had been hidden there. Inside a note read, "*For your babies, Love, Sadie.*" She cried as she touched the cradle.

The cradle was the first item she carried into the cabin. More of her personal things followed, but she gazed at the cradle each time she passed it. Replacing the tarp over her supplies in case it rained during the night, she went inside to fondle and talk to the beautiful cradle. Nothing could have pleased her more. When she looked inside the cradle, she found tiny baby clothes, blankets, and soft materials for making more baby things.

"Oh, Sadie, you wonderful person. Thank you so much," she said. Later, when she went to bed, she placed one hand on the cradle and the other on her stomach.

Up and dressed by sunup, Laura was ready to start the day. Opening all the windows to catch the freshness of the early morning, she gloried in her happy feelings. She filled her cup with coffee and added a spoonful of honey, remembering she was almost out of the sweetener. Could she rob a hive without getting stung?

Taking her coffee, she walked out of the cabin, toward her Widow's Peak and her bench overlooking the river valley. She checked for any animals, friendly or wild, because she had to be careful now considering she was alone again and carried a special treasure under her heart.

Would it be dark like Jim or fair like Rowdy? Would it be a boy or a girl? Thoughts whirled through her mind as she wondered who the father of her baby might be. It came from one of them. Jim had talked to her about being in the family way and wanted her to contact him if she did. However, she did not know which man was the father. Perhaps when the baby was born she would know.

Sometime later, as she finished her breakfast, she heard someone crossing the wooden bridge below the cabin. Hoping it was Matthew but getting her rifle anyway, she went to the door.

Matthew gave her a big hug. "I was thinking I would find you home today. Did you have a safe trip? I worried about you while you were gone."

Laura hugged him as she began telling him the highlights of her trip. "Have you had breakfast?" she asked.

"Oh, yes, we've been enjoying your fresh eggs every morning. Thank you for sharing them with us. But Mother is anxious to leave as soon as possible. I don't want to go. I would rather stay here and work for you. I don't want to live in Georgia."

"I know she has been unhappy here. I'll visit with her tomorrow, and we'll get our arrangements taken care of. Are you ready to work hard today? I have a lot of work for you to do." She led him over to the wagon and began to release the tarp covering.

It took the boy and the pregnant woman until after noon to unload the wagon. Laura wanted things stored just so. Therefore, as Matthew brought boxes in, she worked to unload the items and store them within easy reach.

The most difficult to handle were two large sealed barrels of salted pork and beef. During the winter months, she might not be able to hunt, so she planned to have meat available. They devised a plan to remove some of the meat from each barrel to make it lighter to carry down into the cellar. When they had reloaded the salted meats back into the original barrels, they resealed them.

Matthew laughed when he discovered Laura had purchased a large copper bathtub and filled it with bottles of bathing salts and fragrant soaps. She told him jokingly, "Mind your own business," as she carried her treasures into the cabin.

Near the front of the wagon were large burlap sacks of oats for the horses and colorful sacks of chicken feed. She would use the cloth material to make aprons or shirts when the sacks were empty. Nothing went to waste on a ranch. When the snows came, she would have feed for her animals since the grass would be gone except for what hay she could manage to cut and store in the barn. She wished Matthew could stay to help with the haying, but knew not to voice her wish to him because he would stay. And his mother needed him more.

They worked steadily, not stopping to eat until all the food items had been unloaded. Laura sent Matthew to hitch up the team and unload the remaining sacks of feed, reminding him to put the wagon into the lean-to. She asked him to release the mares into the grassy meadow. While he took care of the animals, Laura went into the cabin to prepare a late dinner of cured ham and fried potatoes.

Matthew gobbled the meal before heading home to continue helping his mother pack. Laura waved from her Widow's Peak as Matthew reached the other side of the valley and waved back at her. Pleased with how well today had gone, she went back in to finish organizing the supplies in the kitchen and to knead the bread dough she would set to rising. She was preparing a going-away basket of food for the Wilsons' journey. She hummed and sang as she worked. She was tired but happy, too. Today had been good, but tomorrow would be even better because she would double the size of her ranch when Mrs. Wilson sold her the 320 acres she owned. She could hardly wait!

The next day, Laura returned to the ranch after noon. She was as pleased as Mrs. Wilson at how well the transaction had gone. Mrs. Wilson expressed her pleasure at the price Laura had insisted on paying for the land. "I would have taken less to get out of there."

After she signed over the deed to Laura, she cried telling her, "This place was always my husband's dream, but it turned into a terrible nightmare we just couldn't wake up from. Nothing has ever been right here. I pray you and your husband will not have the problems we've had."

Laura allowed her to assume Abner was still alive and responded by saying, "Will you take this letter and deed papers to Mr. George Miller in Denver? He is my lawyer who is taking care of business affairs for me. He will record it, making it a legal sale. Here are several letters for Mr. Miller and this letter is to Mr. Little at the bank. It directs him to pay you our agreed upon price. You may want to take just enough money to buy tickets and food for your travels. It isn't a good idea to travel with all of your money. Mr. Little can have the rest transferred to your bank at home. That way you and the children will not lose all your money if by chance something happens. I had robbers try to stop me on the way up."

Mrs. Wilson gasped.

Laura explained, "By the grace of God and a screaming eagle, I made it through. May God continue to protect you and the children as you return home. I'll miss you all." After hugging Mrs. Wilson and each of the children, she mounted her horse. Matthew walked a little way down the trail from the house because he wanted to speak to Laura privately. He asked her again if he could stay and work for her, but she shook her head saying, "Matthew, you are the head of the family now, whether you want to be or not. Your mother is not strong yet, and she is depending on you to help her and the children get back home. I know you will, but I promise you this, when you have her settled and happy again, and when she will let you go, you will always have a job here with me."

"Do you promise?" he asked.

"Yes, it's a promise. If it is one year or several before you return, you will have a job with me." She shook his young hand, slipping a twenty-dollar gold piece into it. "You are worth a lot more than that. Take care of your family and I'll see you when you get back." Laura urged her mare toward home.

CHAPTER 19

While Laura was gone to Denver, Eagle Talon had continued to watch the Spirit Woman's cabin unable to find her. He prayed to the Great Spirit the woman was a good omen. He asked for help from his eagle spirit guide to help him on his vision quest to find buffalo for his people. Without the mighty buffalo, his people would die.

Several days ago, he had slipped down to the cabin. Not sure where she might be, he watched hoping to see her working. He waited for several hours in his hiding place, and then he slipped closer.

Opening the cabin door, he peeped inside. She was not there! With a feeling of relief, he did not encounter her, he moved around the room looking at what odd things the Spirit Woman surrounded herself with. He climbed up a small ladder, which led to a shelf above the corner of the room where she dried her herbs and plants for healing. It pleased him when he recognized plants he used as well. She used powerful medicine. He grunted, pleased with that knowledge.

He wanted something of hers he could use to draw her to him. On the table, she had placed wildflowers in water, which had now drooped and died. She liked flowers. He had seen thorny plants in wooden buckets outside and wondered why she grew them. On a table near her bed, he found a small box and opened it. Inside was an assortment of buttons, hairpins and small shiny trinkets. Picking up each item, he examined it to see if it had the strong power he was seeking. He placed everything back as he'd found it, except one large mother-of-pearl button. He had seen traders from the great waters that brought shells and other treasures like these to swap for furs. It was shiny and beautiful, like her. He hoped she would not miss the possession.

He continued to walk around the cabin a little longer, enjoying the sense of wellbeing he received from being where she lived. He liked her scent, which was everywhere. He needed to know if she could help his people, or if he should stay away from her. He left the cabin as he found it, and prowled around the rest of the buildings.

Soon he returned to the forest following the animal path back to his tepee. Untying the leather strips from one of his braids, he threaded it through the button and tied it in his hair as a coup. He believed he now had power over the Spirit Woman.

～

As he sat cross-legged in the predawn darkness before his fire, his medicine bag and contents spread before him, he breathed the fragrant smoke of the sacred sage filling his lungs and swirling about his head. He chanted a song as he moved his eagle feather fan, motioning the smoke in the four directions to guard him from evil spirits. Today he would take the form of his spirit guide and search for the herds.

As he lit his pipe, filled with his special blend of bearberry, sweet grass, and the powerful peyote, he began his summoning ceremony. He sucked smoke up the long clay pipe into his mouth and lungs, and felt the soothing and comforting relief it gave him. *All will be well* was his last conscious thought as he slipped into a meditative trance.

The rising sun began to chase the dark shadows away as Eagle Talon began his Sunrise Song. When he finished the welcoming song of morning, he sang the Buffalo Song and then made music on his eagle bone whistle. He tapped slowly on his drum as he followed the ancient sacred ceremony calling to his spirit guide.

Suddenly, he felt his spirit transported high above the clouds. His guide had lifted him upward to find the buffalo. He flew in ever-widening circles as the wind currents caught his feathered wings and he soared higher, ever searching.

He cut through the early morning air, his sharp eagle eyes seeing someone driving a wagon into an ambush. Why he flew downward to warn him, he did not know, until the moment the Spirit Woman turned her face upward as he screamed his warning and swooped down. His spirit and hers united together in that moment. His eagle spirit form had not frightened her and his warning was successful. He heard shots, and the wagon continued onward without stopping.

The Spirit Woman had returned! His very soul knew it as if the earth had communicated to him. It had been many suns since he first saw the strange Spirit Woman in the spring. He had not seen her again until today. He sensed she would be able to help him on his quest, but he did not know how or when. He must find out all he could about her.

Now as the sacred sage smoke circled around his head, he suddenly was back on his medicine blanket in his tepee, his eagle spirit had returned him to his human form. He sang a song of thanksgiving for her return as he tapped lightly on his spirit drum.

Eagle Talon rose and broke his fast with water and the remains of a small turkey he had killed and roasted yesterday. He needed to hunt soon for larger game. Later, as he sat outside his tepee, he remembered the time before he came to the mountains. He and his people believed the Great Spirit lived here. He was the medicine man of his tribe, an honor he shared with his mother, Running Fawn. He had sought visions, but they had not come. He had begun to doubt his power as a medicine man.

Running Fawn had sensed a deep loneliness within him which had grown over a period of time. She'd encouraged him to take his tepee into the mountains to fast and pray to the Great Spirit to help him guide the people to the hunting grounds.

At long last, he agreed to go because their hunters continued to return with very little food. Thinking of his mother today, he was amazed at her strength and courage against odds that would overwhelm other people. She seemed to know how to get what she wanted. But it was always for the good of the tribe.

When he left his People, he journeyed two days from their camp to a ridge high above a small valley with a river running through it. He would have water and game here. Pitching his tepee in the protection of a large rock overhang, he spread his warm furs inside. Scooping out a large hole in the center, he'd placed stones around it. After gathering dry wood, he built a fire. His mother had sent dried corn and deer jerky for him to eat. He sat before the fire eating his first meal of the day as the sun went behind the mountains to sleep. For the first time in his life he realized how lonely he was. He did not know what he longed for. But he felt a great void. He knew he could not think of himself when his people would die without buffalo. He would do all in his power to keep it from happening.

CHAPTER 20

The next afternoon, Eagle Talon sat on Spotted Horse hidden in the forest above the valley where he had first seen the Spirit Woman. He hoped she would come and bathe for him again. He liked seeing her strange white body with the straw-colored hair between her legs.

As if in answer to his thoughts, the Spirit Woman moved up the trail where he had first seen her. She was alone this time, without the large wolf. Her hair was bound and she was clothed. Dressed, she appeared to be like any other white woman he had seen walking by the wagons on the prairie. He and his Indian brothers had lain hidden in the tall prairie grasses, as the wagons passed by.

Talon sucked in his breath as he watched her remove her clothes and loosen her long straw colored hair. Stepping nude into the cold spring water, she yelled and splashed under the gentle falls. Eagle Talon and Spotted Horse watched her intently. They stared as the Spirit Woman emerged to get soap to wash her long hair.

After bathing, she stepped from the chilly water, drying her hair with a large cloth as droplets of water ran down her beautiful naked body and pooled at her feet. Talon watched the water glisten and sparkle in the sun. He had never seen anyone else shine so. Was it the water and the sunlight or was it her strong spirit shining through? He felt her spirit call to him. He did not understand why, but her spirit drew him to her. Was it the spirit's way to show him her body so he would not think of the danger? He felt desire for her as a woman, but was this her way to trap a medicine man? He had to be brave and learn all he could about this wild spirit before him.

~

Laura picked up her clothes and walked back to the cabin naked. She enjoyed the feel of the wind kissing her skin and the sensation of the water drying on it. *There's no one around to watch so why do I have to wear clothes if I don't want to?* She enjoyed the freedom.

A strange sensation came over her. She felt a pair of eyes on her body, and she shivered. Whether it was human or animal she did not know, but she ran the rest of the way to the cabin, bolting the door behind her. She had been foolish to walk around nude. There were always hidden dangers lurking in the dark forest.

~

During the night, loud noises on the porch jerked her out of her sleep. Her heart slammed against her chest making it hard to breathe. She listened, trying to figure out if it was sounds coming from outside the cabin or lingering from her dreams. The noises grew louder as someone or something came onto the porch.

The banging, clawing, and growling on the front door brought Laura upright in bed. An angry bear beat on the cabin door and would burst inside any minute. Because she was holding her breath in fear, she almost passed out. Gasping for air, she remembered the cabin door had been built with steel hooks secured by two thick beams barring the door to withstand powerful attacks. What would she have done if he had broken through? Her guns were near the door on a deer antler gun rack. *What a stupid place for her to leave her only protection. She would change their location if she lived through the night.*

Laura heard the firewood, rocking chair, and the dinner bell go flying off the porch—victims of his rage.

Growling and grumbling, he stumbled from the porch as he got closer to the barn and corral she heard the horses scream in terror. The chickens squawked and thrashed about in their cages trying to get out. The barn door had not been built as sturdily as the cabin door, and it cracked under the weight of the bear's assault.

She would not allow the bear to kill any of her livestock. Tampering down her terror, she knew what she had to do. Grabbing her buffalo gun, she made sure it was loaded, then climbed up on the trunk below the window facing in the direction of the barn. Laura slowly eased the shuttered window open. The moon had risen several hours before, providing light for her to see the dark figure of the bear clawing at the barn door in the shadows. She raised her gun, said a prayer that she would kill him outright, and squeezed the trigger. The bear dropped in its tracks. She watched for several more minutes before closing the shutter and bolting it. She'd killed her attacker. She would deal with the carcass in the morning. She was not going out tonight!

~

Hours later, Laura woke to broad daylight. As the memory of last night came flooding back, she chuckled to herself when she realized she had slept with her rifle clutched in her hands. Retracing her steps to the trunk, she cautiously opened the shutters.

"Oh, no!" The bear was not lying dead by the barn door. What would she do with a vicious wounded animal lurking around? Flashbacks of what the Wilsons had endured made her terror grow. Shutting the window, she climbed down trying to think of a plan. It was obvious the bear had not broken into the barn before she dropped him. Had she grazed him, knocking him unconscious for a while? Had he crawled off to wait for her to come out? She had heard stories about animal attacks, but nothing like this had happened to them when Abner was alive. *What should I do now?*

Gathering all her courage, she unbolted the door opening it enough to peer out to see if he was waiting for her. She prayed he had crawled behind the barn and died.

Shrieking and jumping back inside, she slammed the door and bolted it. Her heart raced again in terror. An Indian basket sat outside her door. She regained control of herself, and said aloud, "You're frightened of a basket! But who could have left it?"

Again, she opened the door, peering at the covered basket, recognizing the Ute designs Willow had used. At least it was a comforting sign—or was it? She glanced around at the wreckage the bear had left in his rage. Was an Indian waiting to attack her? They played tricks on people to gain access to their cabins. Seeing no immediate threat, she grabbed the basket, then shut and secured the door.

She set the basket on the table and stared at it for a few minutes. Curiosity overcame fear, as she raised the lid and peered inside. She gasped. Nestled in the basket, surrounded by wet leaves to keep it cool, sat a large heart. On top of the heart was one long claw. She had killed the grizzly! Someone had taken it and offered her the heart as a token of her kill. But, she thought with a shiver, *who left me the heart?*

She stood several more minutes, concentrating on a number of possibilities, but each time she returned to the knowledge that it was someone from Willow's tribe. It was someone who was strong enough to process it, because a slight person could not have managed the large carcass. She had heard from others that bear meat was delicious. She decided to find out for herself. She lifted the heart from the basket, washed it, and cut it up into smaller pieces. A delicious stew for her supper tonight would be wonderful. At least she did not have to worry about a wounded bear. But who could be lurking in the forest watching her? She would keep her guns even closer from now on. And no more nude bathing.

She built a fire and hung the pot over it to simmer all day. She would add herbs and fresh vegetables later. She licked her lips in anticipation of the feast.

She repaired the damage to the porch as best she could, talked to the horses and chickens as she let them out of their pens, and watered her garden as she gathered early vegetables to can. Her garden was producing. Since the Wilsons left, she did not have anyone close to share with.

Soon, she would have to tell her friends about Abner's death and the baby. She went over in her mind what she would say and how to say it. When she did go to Everclear, she would not go near the trading post. She had supplies from Denver and she would never buy anything from Tuffy again. However, she wanted Tuffy to know she had come to Everclear without visiting his establishment. She would visit Cora and the girls, take them eggs and vegetables to enjoy, and then she would tell them about Abner and the baby. Nothing spread as fast as gossip from a whorehouse.

With a happy heart, Laura opened the cabin door the next morning to find a larger covered basket on her porch. She searched the area for her benefactor. Seeing no one, she dragged the heavy basket inside. She raised the lid and saw a hindquarter of bear meat. It was cut into pieces with the bone removed, making it easier for her to manage. Whoever took the carcass, was sharing the meat with her. The goodwill offering pleased her.

Slicing off several pieces to fry later, she stored the rest in the cold cellar. She would enjoy it as long as she could before canning it for the winter. Bear meat would be nutritious for her as the baby grew. She would not have to worry as much about meat when the snows came. A fear seeped in about being alone during the winter, but she moved her thoughts to the chores for the day. She had helped a woman on the wagon train have a baby so at least she had an idea of what was to come. Could she do it alone? She tried not to worry about it, deciding to plan out what to do when the time drew closer.

CHAPTER 21

*E*agle Talon was very busy after the Spirit Woman shot the bear. He'd heard the explosion of the buffalo gun echoing throughout the valley. Hurrying through the darkened forest, he hid near the cabin to investigate. He could smell the scent of gunpowder in the air, but did not know what she shot. Hearing a whinny from one of the horses down in the barn, he turned in that direction and saw a large dark form slumped against the barn door.

Now, on the second day, he was riding Spotted Horse and leading his packhorse pulling a travois loaded with bear meat, he gave the huntress the heart as her prize for the kill. It would give her strength and the spirit of the bear would guard her. He left her a large part of one of the legs as well. Knowing the grizzly would be too large for her, he'd decided to take the rest to his people. Time was slipping by, and he had not been able to find the buffalo, but perhaps the bear meat was a beginning of a good omen.

Eagle Talon felt himself grin. His mother would tan the bear skin for him and he would give it to the Spirit Woman to cover her bed in the cold months to come. Perhaps she would invite him to lie under it with her. *Where had that thought come from?* He must not think of her in such way. He did not know if she was good or bad medicine for him. His spirit had connected with her spirit in ways he could not explain. He continued toward his village with the cooled bear meat he had hung in the tree overnight, wrapped in wet leaves, and covered with the fur.

When the village came into his sight, he urged his stallion to move faster. He wanted to talk with his mother and his grandfather, Smoking Owl. He needed their council regarding the Spirit Woman.

A crowd gathered about Eagle Talon as he slid from his horse and proudly showed off the bearskin and the meat. Sounds of approval were heard as he talked of his vision quest and finding the bear left by a white hunter. His mother divided the meat among the families to begin processing it. Hungry eyes gazed upon the meat as the women went to work.

Talon carried the fur into his mother's tepee. She turned on him as the flap closed. "Now tell me the truth about the bear," she demanded.

He hooted at her, saying, "I cannot fool you, can I? I went on the vision quest, as you wanted. I have not had the dreams of the buffalo, but I did find a Spirit Woman. It is she who has provided the meat."

Running Fawn studied her first born, "What do you mean she has provided the meat?"

"The angry bear attacked her and she killed him with her long rifle. She is too small to eat all the meat so I left her enough for her needs and brought the rest here to you. I would like for you to tan the hide as a gift for her." He sat cross-legged near the fire, noticing for the first time the bear's missing ear. *I wonder how that happened?*

After several moments of silence his mother softly asked, "Does this Spirit Woman have hair the color of dry grass in the hot summer?"

Talon should not have been amazed at her knowledge, for she, too, was a spiritual leader of the tribe. He nodded. He would not meet her eyes for fear she would see all his thoughts about the Spirit Woman.

"I have had dreams about a woman with long, straw-colored hair who speaks to animals. Does she speak to animals?" she asked.

A strangled sound came from his lips as he tried to clear his throat to answer her, "I have seen a silver wolf come at her call and dance around and kiss her. Even Spotted Horse, who will not obey anyone but me, wants to go to her. It is as if she calls to both of us."

"My dreams have been unclear about her. She could be good medicine or bad medicine for you and for our tribe. You must be careful until you know. When will you go back, my son?" she asked knowing even now he yearned to return.

"I will leave in three suns," he said to his mother.

"I want us to pray and sing to the Great Spirit to bring us the buffalo and a good harvest before you go. Our people cannot remain in this place long without food and better shelter. Even though it is early summer, we see signs telling us this winter will be bad," Running Fawn told him.

Talon left early on the third day, anxious to get back to the Spirit Woman. He still did not know why, but he wanted to be nearby, watching her.

~

On the same day Talon began his trip back, Laura left the cabin before dawn to ride to Everclear. Leading her packhorse with a basket of eggs packed in straw and a number of other baskets filled with fresh vegetables, she rode hard, wanting to get there and back before dark.

Hours later, she reined the horses in at Cora's. Beating on the front door, it took a while before it was opened by a sleepy Hank who was not pleased to see her.

"Hello, Hank. Would you tell Cora I am here to visit with her, please? And I have eggs and produce on the packhorse. Would you please bring it in?"

"She hasn't been to bed but a short time. Will be none too happy to be woke up," he grumbled.

"I know, but please tell her I need to talk with her."

Fifteen minutes later, Cora made her sleepy grand entrance in another wild flowered lacy wrapper.

She gave Laura a big hug and motioned for her to sit down.

"I brought you and the girls some produce and eggs from the ranch. I had Hank unload it. But I wanted to visit and find out how you all were."

"Oh Laura, I am glad you came. Something wonderful has happened to me. I received a letter from a lawyer in Denver, a Mr. Miller. His letter said I'd inherited a nice hotel in a good location there. I couldn't believe someone's generosity to an old whore." She wiped tears with her lace handkerchief.

"That's wonderful, Cora. Who did it? One of your gentleman callers? An old love? Oh, tell me quick."

Sniffing, Cora whispered, "That's the strange thing. The letter said it was anonymous. The hotel and a bank account are in my name. I can do whatever I want with it. I can sell it or I can live there and run it as a hotel or a whorehouse. My choice, the letter said."

"Cora isn't it what you always wanted? A place of your own? If you want a different life, now you can be respectable—or not," Laura said crying with Cora. "How soon will you be leaving?"

"I'm not sure. Two of the girls want to go with me, and the others don't. I'm confused about what to do. Any suggestions?"

"When I worked for you, you told me how much you wanted out of the business. Here's your chance. If the girls going with you want out, then take them. The others can stay here or go somewhere else."

"For someone so young, you're so wise. You're right to remind me that this is what I've prayed for. And, yes, whores do pray."

"Oh, Cora, I know you pray. I also know you're one of the kindest and nicest women I have ever had the pleasure to know. When are you leaving? Your new life is waiting!" Laura hugged Cora again. "But before you pack, I need to tell you and the girls something that's happened. Will you call them down so I only have to explain it once?"

It wasn't long before the six sleepy whores were assembled around Laura in the parlor. She stood up, pacing the floor as each sleepy-faced woman watched her.

"You all know the details of what happened to me the first time I came alone to the settlement to buy supplies. The results proved to be in my favor since Cora was gracious enough to give me a job and safe place to stay. I couldn't go back to the ranch for a week until I could steal my horses back and get home. Well, when I made it home, Abner was upset with me. He accused me of all kinds of vile things and even threatened to beat me, but when I got his attention, I told him what happened. He couldn't believe what Tuffy had done. He started walking around, cussing, and yelling about how Tuffy shouldn't have attacked a married woman, especially not with an audience. He kept working himself up about Tuffy stealing my horses making it so I couldn't come home and take care of him. He was a sick man and needed me to help him. I tried to get him to settle down, but he kept on yelling and pacing. He was disappointed because he'd trusted Tuffy all these years and this is how he repaid him. He quickly tired and sat down in the rocking chair. Looking at me, he said, 'Laura, I'm sorry.' And he died right there!" She squeezed tears from her eyes as she glanced at her audience to see the effect.

"He died? Just like that? When did it happen?" Cora asked.

"The day I got back. I didn't know what to do with him being dead and all. I...I couldn't leave him sitting in the rocking chair, so I dug a hole. It took me hours to dig it by myself," she whispered, as she covered her face with her hands and wept.

"I couldn't tell anyone about his death the last time I was here because then it would have made it real. I tried to pretend it hadn't happened, but it did."

Cora jumped up and put her arms around Laura and Hanna patted her back. She let them comfort her for a while then Laura finally said, "Since it happened, I've had several months to learn to live alone. I will be staying on the ranch and doing my best to run it."

Cora poured Laura a cup of coffee from the pot Hank had bought into the parlor. "I sense there is more you want to tell us. Am I right?"

Laura dropped her head as she wiped her tears and answered, "Yes, Cora, there is more. Abner may have passed away, but he did leave me with a little present. I am going to have a baby. I found out recently so I still can't believe it's happened."

"A baby! Oh how wonderful! But wait, you can't live out there by yourself with a baby. How will you manage? Who will protect you?" Cora wailed at Laura.

"Thank you for your concern, but please try to understand my situation. I have nowhere else to go. Now you know why it's been so important for me to save the ranch. I thank God every day he provided the two gold nuggets. Now I have a home for my child. When the winter snows come, I will have food. I killed a bear last week and I've been canning the meat," she told them proudly.

The women and Hank, who had been listening, stared at her in amazement. Cora squeaked out, "You killed a bear? Why? How?"

"It tried to come into the cabin one night, but couldn't bust the door down. Then it went down to the barn to get to the animals. I shot it with Abner's buffalo gun, and it dropped dead. It may have been from fright since the gun makes a horrible noise. Either way, I have plenty of meat now." She grinned at their stunned expressions. "If you tell anyone about the bear, please mention I will shoot whomever comes snooping around my ranch. I am on the watch for the outlaws Tuffy sent after me, too."

Cora and the women almost swooned upon hearing about the outlaws. Laura hoped each one would spread her bear story and the cause of her husband's death.

"One more bit of information for all of you. This will be the last time I come to Everclear. I can't safely buy supplies from Tuffy since he has made it clear he hates all women and especially me. But when I go to Denver, I will look you up. I want to stay in touch with each of you," Laura whispered tearfully as she hugged them farewell. She even got a hug from Hank.

Laura left, riding hard for her ranch. She watched her back trail in case Tuffy heard she was in town and had sent out any henchmen again. She returned to her cabin, bolted the door, and breathed a sigh of relief. She was tired from the long ride, but happy she had let her friends know about the baby.

~

Weeks passed as Laura drove herself hard to preserve the vegetables from her garden and any wild berries she found in the forest. Early one morning, she opened the cabin door to find a basket full of wild strawberries sitting on the porch. Her benefactor had returned, but she did not see anyone nearby.

Picking up the basket, she sampled a few as she placed it on the table. She would make jam later in the day. It would be delicious with the bread she had baking. "I think I'll leave an offering out and see if this person likes bread and jam," she said, and started at the sound of her own voice. She'd had no one to talk to since she left Cora's.

The next morning, the bread and wild strawberry jam were replaced with a clay container filled with wild honey and honeycomb. Delighted, she picked it up and danced inside. For supper, she prepared a thick bear stew with garden vegetables and a pan of cornbread. She placed a large serving in a pot to keep it hot, sliced a portion of her cornbread, and wrapped it in a dishtowel. She placed the items on the rail of the porch as it began to grow dark, dashed back into the cabin, and bolted the door.

The next morning the empty pot and folded towel lay in front of the door. She was delighted as she picked them up. It appeared her benefactor enjoyed her cooking. She watched the forest edge for any signs of movement. Seeing none, she turned back inside to start her long day.

~

Eagle Talon watched as the Spirit Woman searched the forest. Still unsure of her effect on him, he waited cautiously. He liked her food. He liked the game they were playing. It pleased him to have a woman preparing food for him.

His thoughts were about the Spirit Woman as he left to go hunting. He decided to kill a deer and share the fresh meat with her. He liked giving the Spirit Woman gifts. She seemed to be pleased each time he left her something and, in return, she shared her food with him. He liked the taste of her food and wondered while he lay alone at night how she might taste. He hoped to find out soon.

CHAPTER 22

*E*arly the next day, Laura began cutting the grassy hay in the meadow behind her cabin. It was thick and luscious even with the horses grazing on it. She prayed her strength held out. She needed the hay for the mares and the cow during the winter. She had plenty to do and not much time to do it. With summer nearly over, the warm days grew shorter, and the long nights had begun to cool.

Laura swung the sickle from side to side cutting the meadow grass. She would leave it to dry for a few days before she gathered it in the wagon and hauled it to the barn. She worked steadily most of the morning, but she would have to stop soon. Working as hard as she could, she cut three long rows the width of the sickle. She heard a horse whinny from the ridge above her and glanced up.

Sensing she was being watched, she stopped her work. Scanning the ridge and trees, her hand moved to rest on her holster. She listened to the birds in the forest as they continued their tweeting. All was quiet. Soon she relaxed and went back to cutting the tall grass. She cut another row before quitting for the day. She had other chores she would need her strength for. She walked toward the cabin, leaving the sickle in the field where she had stopped.

For supper, Laura fried slices of some fresh deer meat her unseen benefactor had left her. She said a prayer to the Lord for the blessings of the food He provided, and asked Him to watch over Jim and Rowdy, keeping them safe, and then she ate her solitary meal.

After a tiring and busy afternoon of chores, she ate her light supper and then cleaned the kitchen. Laura liked to write in her journal each evening before going to bed. It was a quiet and relaxing part of her day to think of all the simple pleasures she enjoyed. The peace and quietness of the serene mountains, sounds of the gurgling spring, tall green pines, and aspen whispering to each other in the breeze added to her sense of well-being. When she did go to her lonely bed, she relived her one glorious night with the two angel men who had come and gone in her life. One of them left something very special behind. As she placed her hands on her rounding belly, she thanked them both for their love. A sudden flutter under her hands startled her. The baby had shifted, and she felt it! What a wonderful feeling! She fell asleep with her hands resting on her treasure.

The next morning when she went to the meadow, all of the hay had been cut and the sickle leaned against a tree. Questions flew through her mind at the hard work that was done in one night. She would be able to rake the hay in a few days to store in the barn. *Who could have done such a special thing? My mysterious benefactor?* She scanned the forest again for him.

Seeing no one, she picked up the sickle and returned to the cabin. Since she did not have the laborious work to do anymore, she decided it would be great to fish and rest. The day was warm and sunny as she headed to the river with her fishing pole. Laura sat down on a rock near the river and cast her line into the rushing water. She could already smell the fried trout for supper. Her mouth watered at the thought.

Waiting by the stream for a trout to take the bait, she heard a horse galloping on the ridge high above her. It seemed to be following the narrow trail where she searched for her healing plants. Looking upward, she saw in a flash a white-spotted horse and rider racing between the trees. She heard a yell and a loud thud as if something hit the hard ground.

Laura jumped up and raced up the lane to the cabin as fast as she could. She grabbed her bag of herbs, and started out on the forest trail.

When she came around a small bend in the path, a beautiful spotted horse stood over a man who lay on his back, motionless. As she approached, the horse turned and came at Laura with bared teeth. To protect herself, she hit him square on the nose with her right fist as hard as she could.

When her fist met his nose, it set him down hard on his rear end as his back legs slid out from under him on the mossy path. She glared shaking her finger at him, "If you attack me again, I will hit you harder. Now get up and help me with your master." She stepped around the stunned horse, walking to the injured rider. Behind her, she heard the horse get up, and shake himself. As she bent over the rider, the horse came up behind her leaning over her shoulder. He nickered softly. "Males! They are all alike. Treat them rough and they respect you." She scoffed and pushed the horse out of her way.

The man lying on the ground was an Indian. But his features were unlike anyone Laura had ever seen. The oval shaped head surrounded by the thick black hair shiny as a raven's wing was braided into two long braids that reached passed his shoulders. She touched the bridge of his shapely nose, which was almost "hawk-like" as she continued downward tracing his lips with her finger. Greatly enjoying the feel of his skin beneath her fingers. The hue of his skin was a dark brown instead of the reddish browns she had seen on other Indians. The rawhide holding his breech-cloth in place had broken, exposing his maleness. She was surprised at how well-endowed he was. Of course, she had only seen two other men from which to pass judgment, but he was bigger than they were. She wondered inappropriately, *when he gets excited does it stay the same or grow?*

Shaking herself, she came back to the present situation and drew the loincloth over his privates so she could concentrate on his injuries.

It appeared he struck a tree limb as he galloped along the path. His chest had scrapes and cuts from the rough bark. He fell backward from his horse, striking the ground. She lifted his head, feeling his neck bones carefully; making sure his neck was not broken. Warm blood wet her fingers. She could easily stop the bleeding on the cut, but she worried he might have a brain injury. She hoped not. Taking clean cloths and herbs from her bag, she wrapped his head to stop the blood flow. Then she began to examine the rest of his body for broken bones.

As she felt down his left side and along his leg, she noticed a stirring under his loincloth. *Oh please. Even when unconscious, they react to a woman's touch!* When she examined the other side, his penis rose up. Well, now she knew what it would do when aroused even by accident. It was longer and thicker as she struggled to cover it with the loincloth.

Did she want this stranger as she had wanted Jim and Rowdy? *What is wrong with me?*

Laura knew she could not leave him on the damp ground with only his loincloth as cover. Standing up, she noticed for the first time a hidden footpath leading off the well-worn animal route. The spotted horse followed her until she came into an open area where a tepee stood in the middle of a small clearing.

She opened the flap and ventured inside where she found a bed with Indian blankets, furs, and buckskin clothing. Various baskets and pottery jars decorated with the same designs of the items left at her door were near the fire pit in the middle of the tepee. "So this must be where my benefactor lives." She looked around, pondering what to do next.

Making a decision, she picked up his blankets and some rawhide strings. She emerged from the tepee, pushing the horse out of her way. She spotted a travois lying near the edge of the clearing. This was what he had used to transport his tepee, and now she would use it to move him. Before long, she figured out how to harness the horse to it and led him down the path to his injured rider.

Several hours later, she had the injured man in his tepee. She debated on whether to take him to her cabin or his tepee, but the path to her cabin was steep, and his tepee was only a short distance away. She'd had a tough time getting him moved, but the horse was a big help. Laura told him what she wanted him to do and he stood patiently while she managed to roll the injured man onto the travois. The horse then walked slowly to the clearing, dragging his load. The hardest part had been figuring out how to get the large man into the tepee. She rolled him off the travois and into a sitting position against the door opening. Then she managed to push him head first into the opening onto some furs. After crawling over him to get into the tepee, she pulled and tugged him until she had the rest of him inside.

Spreading out blankets along his long torso, she again rolled him over until she had him off the ground, securely nestled in his buffalo robe. Totally exhausted from all the pulling and tugging, she stopped to rest.

She took the blankets off the travois wiping as much dirt and mud off as possible before covering him with them. She would bring clean blankets from the cabin when she went to get warm clothes and food for herself. She checked his head wound, pleased to see it had stopped bleeding. She made sure he was warm and left the tepee.

Spotted Horse followed her down the path like a lap dog. She heard him clopping along behind her and was glad he was willing to follow because she would use him to transport items she could not carry back to the camp. He waited outside while she rounded up the things she would need for the night. She placed them in two large Indian baskets and secured them with rope across the horse's back. She put live coals in her cast iron stewpot so she could carry it back to the tepee. She would build a fire before dark with those. Taking her rifle and latching the door to the cabin as she left, she took hold of the rope on the large spotted horse and led him back to his master.

~

Shadows danced on the walls of the tepee. Talon's eyes blinked open and closed as he tried to remember how he had gotten here. *Am I dreaming? Am I dead? What happened?* His head hurt so much he could not think. He moaned. A sound nearby caught his attention as one of the shadows came closer to him. Straw-colored hair fell across the furs as a cool hand rested on his forehead.

The Spirit Woman! He must be dreaming she was in his tepee. He liked her touch. It soothed him, as he knew it would. He moaned again when she removed it. "Does your head ache? Will you drink something?" she murmured in a sleep-laden voice. His throat was dry. He could do nothing but nod.

She cradled his head between her firm breast and one arm as she offered him water with the other. She smelled of flowers. After he quenched his thirst, she gave him willow bark tea sweetened with honey. He wanted to ask her so many questions, but sleep overcame him as she laid his head back onto the soft furs.

~

Laura cared for him for four days and nights. He did not seem to be getting any better and she was concerned he might die. She had not been able to get much soup or willow bark tea down him before he would drift off again. His body burned with high fever and she resorted to bathing him with cool water as often as she could. His maleness responded to her as she bathed his fevered body. She put cold water on it making it docile.

At those times, she burned, wanting to make love to him. He was a powerful man. It may have been him who had been watching her cutting the meadow hay. He must have left the food at her door. Had that been his way of courting her? She did not know Indian customs, but if he ever woke up, she would soon find out.

Before dawn on the fifth day, he woke, and Laura was able to get more food and tea down him than ever before. He reached up and touched her breast. She gasped. With a grin on his handsome face, he fell back asleep.

Since he had not died and now seemed to be improving, thoughts began to swirl in her head. *Was he lusty? How did Indians make love? Was it different from white people?* When he woke again, she was sure she would find out. Thankful his fever had broken, she left him to do her daily chores with the aim of returning to check on him later in the day. She hoped he would get better. He was such a handsome man even if he was an Indian. *Could he speak English?* She hoped so because her Ute was limited.

Entering the tepee later in the day, she jumped when a husky male voice asked, "What is your name?"

"Oh, you're awake. Good. How do you feel? Are you hungry? Is your fever back?" She drew near to his pallet and placed her hand on his forehead.

He grabbed her wrist with surprising strength, pulling her down to him, "What is your name, woman?"

She stared at his full lips and the curve of his chin before answering, "My name is Laura. What's your name?"

"I am Eagle Talon. You have been caring for me?"

She nodded waiting for him to release her arm.

"Thank you for helping me. I am a medicine man and I dream dreams. I have dreamed of you," he said.

She gasped louder and tried to pull away from him but he would not release her.

Instead he pulled her down onto his pallet and into his embrace. "What happens between a warrior and his Spirit Woman is for their joy."

"Why do you call me Spirit Woman?"

"The first time I saw you, you were coming up out of the water and your beautiful body glistened. Your spirit called to my spirit at that very moment. When you spoke, a wild wolf came to you. It was powerful medicine, Spirit Woman," he said in awe as he pulled her tighter against his hard body.

"You saw me bathing? Were you watching from the ridge? I could feel hungry eyes upon me but couldn't see you." At least now, she knew who had watched her.

"I had not felt desire for a long time. I came on a vision quest for my people to find buffalo and instead found you. I was not sure if you were human or spirit but you kept drawing me back. I have watched and waited to see if you had a man to love you and take care of you. I have not seen any man. Do you have a warrior who has spoken for you?"

She pushed herself up to a sitting position so she could look into his eyes. "Many years ago I was forced to marry a man who took me away from my family and brought me to this wilderness. He died earlier in the summer, leaving me with child. I don't have a man, but I don't need one. I can take care of myself."

"I know you can. I have watched you trying to ready yourself and your unborn child for the winter that is to come, but maybe you will help me find something I can do for you," he reached up to softly touch her face and her lips. She leaned into his hand at the gentle touch.

"Will you let me see you as you were at the spring?"

She stood above him and released her hair from its braids allowing it to flow around her. Never taking her eyes from his, she unbuttoned her work shirt. As she dropped her clothing, she liked the lusty looks he gave her, knowing he was enjoying all he was seeing.

When she stood before him naked, she could feel his eyes burning into her flesh. She stared back at him thinking about what would happen next.

He drew back the furs covering his lower body. Her eyes feasted upon his manhood long and thick as it leaned forward, slapping his stomach in jerking motions.

Offering her his hand, he guided her to straddle him.

Touching one breast and then the other, he pulled her forward to him so he could fondle and lick each one in turn as she moaned her pleasure and arched her back at his actions.

Inching backward, she encountered the tip of his engorged manhood and pushed it into her hot wetness. She moaned her pleasure at his touch.

Her continued motion helped her to impale herself on him. His moans told her he liked what she was doing to his rigid member. Because of his length, she took her time mounting him. She had learned from Jim and Rowdy what to do, but neither of them had been this size.

At a mounting rush of passion, she called out, "Yes, yes, oh yes," as she worked faster up and down on him. He held her tightly as she writhed in her climax.

Regaining her direction, she pumped up and down on him again, "You please me very much." He liked what she said as he pushed even deeper.

She breathed softly into his ear, brushed her breasts across his chest, and continued in a smooth rhythm with him, "I never thought I would be able to take all of you. You feel wonderful, my strong warrior."

Talon grabbed her buttocks as he pushed into her. She took the initiative and rode him faster, hoping he would not be harmed because of his head injury. She rode him hard. She was his Spirit Woman and he was her Warrior.

She whispered encouraging words to him and he whispered Ute words to her. She told him, "Do you like what I'm doing to you?"

He nodded.

"Well, come on then show me how well you like me," She increased her actions and he followed her lead, giving as much as he had. As their intense climaxes consumed them, it seemed the tepee went up in flaming fire and smoke.

Talon held her against his chest. "Do not leave me, Spirit Woman. I like this feeling of being one with you. I have longed for you from the beginning," he whispered into her hair.

Minutes passed as he soon regained his desire moving in and out of her again, as he held onto her tightly. She felt him growing hard again deep inside her.

Talon hushed her. "Be quiet and let me love you gently," He continued to slowly push in and out of her.

"We didn't kiss each other," she said with wonder as she softly touched his handsome face.

"What is a kiss?" he asked.

"Let me show you." She placed light kisses on his face until she reached his mouth. She moved her lips on his. When he opened his mouth, she slipped her tongue inside. She knew he liked the feeling because when she circled her tongue around in his mouth, she felt a response between her legs. It seemed impossible, but it encouraged him to give her more. She matched her rhythm to his, letting him set the pace this time. Whispered encouragements mingled with increased breathing as their passion reached to the heavens. With a loud scream of pleasure from Laura, Talon released his seed deep within her as they both frightened the wildlife in the forest with their yells of wild abandon and passion.

As they lay together, happy and sated, she asked, "Why are you here alone?"

"My people are Ute. I am their medicine man and spirit leader as is my mother. I have been on a vision quest," he said turning her over on her right side as he pulled her left leg over his hip. He refused to release her.

"Oh, what is happening to me?" as he turned a pale green and grabbed his head.

"You shouldn't have raised your head because you have a bad head wound. You were injured by a fall from your horse about five days ago. Please lie back down and you'll feel better. I will get you a cool cloth." She rose to fetch cool water and a cloth.

"I did not fall from my horse. I am a great warrior," he mumbled proudly when she returned to his side.

"You may be a great warrior, but you still fell from your horse when you hit a low limb." She smiled at his angry expression. "I feel bad now for making love to you when you're still so ill. Please don't die because of it."

"I will not die now. I will grow stronger because of it. I will help you do whatever it is you need done when I recover."

"I've been working the ranch myself, trying to keep it together and winter is coming. We will be fine. We don't need any help from you or anyone."

He said no more on the subject as he drifted off to sleep again. His last thought was, "We shall see what you need from me."

Talon quickly recovered from his head injuries. Laura fussed over him, making him rest often.

After the first encounter of sleeping with him, she went willingly to his bed. He seemed to thrive from her loving him. He was a strong powerful man and a lusty lover. What he did not know, he was willing to learn. He showed her new tricks, and she showed him some new ones, too. He seemed to like the kissing aspect, wanting to practice on her all the time and all over her body. She was ready and willing.

She was not lazy. She worked hard every day. His eyes were constantly on her and she watched him as well. If they touched at any time, it wasn't long before they were entangled in passion. As Talon improved, Laura spent more time in her cabin. He was quick to join her there.

As she grew larger, her pants were not fitting in the waist. She tied them up with a small rope because she could no longer button them. The baby now was active at night; when she lay down to rest, the child would not be still. She always thought of the baby as he. She hoped it would be a boy, someone to leave the ranch to someday. She had many plans for herself, her child, and the ranch. The first time Talon felt the baby move, his eyes widened in amazement. After that he often laid his hand on her stomach.

One day while tending to her cabin, Laura opened the cabin door, startled to see Talon standing there with a large buck thrown over his shoulder. He said in an irritated voice, "Where is my horse? I had to hunt without him."

She said sweetly, "I put him in a stall to feed him grain. He's been so hungry."

In a strangled voice he yelled, "You have been feeding my warhorse. No one feeds or cares for my horse, but me. What have you done to him?" He dropped the deer on the porch and headed for the barn, Laura on his heels.

Leading the horse out of the barn, he said to Laura in a tone that should have frightened her but did not, "Do not touch my horse! He is bad medicine for you. He will hurt you. Do you understand?"

"I put him in there to keep him out of my way while I work."

"Out of your way? Woman, what are you talking about? This is a warhorse and he does not get in your way," he roared.

She stood, looking up at him in defiance. "Yes, he does. Turn him loose and you'll see he follows me everywhere."

Talon released the horse. Laura turned her back on both of them heading for the cabin. She peeked over her shoulder. The horse followed her. When she stopped, he stopped. When she moved, he moved. If she bent over to pick up a bucket, he leaned over her to see what she was doing. Laura turned to Talon and said, "Do you see why I put him in the barn? He's a pest when I am working. Oh, are you going to skin that deer?" She hurried to the cabin before she laughed aloud at his confusion over her changing the subject.

A woman and a horse had outsmarted Talon. For the first time in a long time, he grinned. Then he started to laugh until he had tears in his eyes. His amazing woman had conquered his warhorse, and she had conquered the warrior as well.

Picking up the deer, he began the skinning process. Laura would prepare a wonderful meal for them to enjoy together with the fresh meat. She would be sad when he broke the news he had to leave. His people needed him now, but he knew she needed him as well. As he worked, he prayed to the Great Spirit to help him do the right thing for Laura and his people.

After skinning, cleaning, and cutting up the deer in sizes Laura would be able to handle, he waited for her to go to the barn to close up the animals for the night. He caught her, pulling her into an empty stall where he had put fresh hay earlier. Pushing her up against the feed trough, he kissed and fondled her. Putting pressure on her shoulders, he eased her down to her knees before him and pulled his loincloth aside.

Taking him in both hands, she fondled him as she sinuously kissed him along his long length working toward his sensitive area. When she reached it, he was rock hard. She slipped him into her hot mouth and began to suck loudly on him. Standing with both legs apart, he twisted his hands in her long hair, holding on for the ride.

Gasping, he said, "Pull your pants down, woman. I need you now!"

Not releasing him with her mouth, she stood up enough to slip her pants down and wiggled out of them. Spreading the pants behind her on the hay to lay on, she tugged on him to bring him to his knees as she continued to kiss and suck.

Her mouth released him and as she lay back, he put his long finger into her to see if she was wet for him.

"I'm always ready for you, my lusty lover," she said.

He pushed into her waiting hotness as she spread her legs and wrapped them around him, not wanting to let him go.

CHAPTER 23

*T*alon left at first light. He had packed his belongings before going hunting the day before. He told Laura after they had eaten supper in her cabin that he would be leaving to tend to his tribe. He explained he had to return to his people because winter was approaching and they needed to find a place with protection and food.

"Where will they go?" she said concerned for his people.

"Right now they are camped on the outer plains, but when the cold wind blows they must have warm shelter and food. We have searched many moons for the buffalo but they are gone. My people have not had a chance to prepare for winter," he told her sadly as he explained the problems and his disappointment in himself as their medicine man.

"I know of a small hidden valley on my land where your people could live and be safe for the winter. I have food I will share with them," she said.

He stared at her in awe, "You are offering my people shelter and food? Why?"

"They are your people and I know how you worry about their welfare. You have a responsibility to keep your tribe safe. You've helped me, please let me help you," she answered.

Unable to control their passion for each other, they shed their clothes and begin to explore each other's bodies before the warmth of the fireplace. He knelt before her and kissed a fiery path down to the apex between her legs.

He spread her lower lips with his thumbs and placed tender kisses on her throbbing essence. She grasped his head pulling him closer to herself moaning, "Yes, yes!" His long tongue darted in and out as she encouraged him with her cries and the movement of her hips.

Carrying her to the bed, he placed her on the quilt her mother had made her. He knelt between her legs as if before her throne to worship her. Continuing to pleasure her with his tongue, he suckled her until she was weeping and crying from the pure pleasure he was giving her.

When she shouted her release, he lay down beside her as he began to worship her body with his hands and lips. She sighed as he drew heartily on one of her breasts, playing with the other with his thumb and forefinger. His hand passed over her swollen tummy and she gasped.

"Have I hurt you?" he asked concern in his voice.

"No. I will be much bigger when you return. Will you still want me like this?" she asked thinking she might lose him.

"I claim the fruit of your womb as mine. Why would I not want you as well as the baby? Do not worry because it will not matter to me. Now love me like a woman loves her husband who is going away for a while," he said passionately to her.

She heard the word husband and wondered if he was thinking they would marry someday. She knew she would never marry again, but now was not the time to address the issue. She wanted him and he wanted her. That was the most important thought at the moment.

He continued to kiss his way down past her rounding belly, lavishing attention again on her private parts.

She loved what he did to her and it did not take him long to bring her to fulfillment again with sighs and moans of pleasure coming from her as she thrashed on the bed. He was pleased at how she readily responded to him.

When she came back down, he was still kneeling between her legs appearing pleased with himself. Reaching up and taking him into her hand, she guided him toward the place his lips had been. He watched as she spread her legs wider to accommodate him as his tip touched the mouth of her waiting wetness. He began to lower himself into her. She was soft, hot, and waiting as he inched his way into her. She sighed her displeasure anytime he withdrew from her which made him smile warmly. She wanted more of him and he was happy to give it to her.

He eased into her again, ever mindful of the baby growing in her. Supporting most of his weight on his arms, he continued to push into her. She thrashed and moaned, "Don't stop! Harder now," as he pushed in and out of her. When her thrashings ended, she opened her eyes and looked at him. "Oh, my darling, it was wonderful," she told him breathlessly.

He continued to move back and forward, "You will give me much pleasure before this night is done." His movements soon began to build, and he rode her harder and faster. She abandoned all control as she helped him. He was bellowing at the top of his lungs and she was screaming for him not to stop when the world around them seemed to shatter like millions of falling stars.

After a few minutes, he rolled to his side, taking her with him as he pulled her leg over his. He kissed her lips and whispered words to her in his language from his heart. She did not understand the words but she sensed the feelings.

He switched back to English as he told her how much she pleased him and what a wonderful lover she was. He hoped he had pleased her too. She nodded her head. She had been loved to perfection and the night was still young. What a night of pleasure it turned out to be!

Talon left quietly before the sun was up. Laura slept so peacefully he did not have the heart to wake her. He did not want a tearful goodbye either. He wanted her to remember the hours they had spent loving each other. His heart was joyful as he took one last look at her sweet angelic face asleep on the pillow and remembered her continued passion for him during the night. He placed logs on the dying coals so she would wake to a warm cabin. Silently he said to her, *"I will return as soon as I can. Be brave and be safe, my love."* Then he was gone.

He traveled fast and late into the evening before finding a rock shelter from the high wind that had begun to blow cold during the afternoon.

Building a fire, he roasted a grouse he shot with his bow and arrow earlier. His head was hurting again so he prepared a mixture of herbs and willow bark to ease the pain. He hobbled Spotted Horse, allowing him to graze during the night and keep watch for wolves and bears.

After he had eaten and taken his medicine, he began to feel better. Wrapping his blanket around himself, he lay down near the fire to sleep. As the fire died down, a pair of blue eyes watched him from the forest. The wolf did not attack the sleeping man, only guarded him as he slept as Laura had asked him to.

Talon dreamed. His people were crying, talking, and moving. He could not see where they were going. In his dream, they moved the village; but why and where? Buffalo were on the plains grazing as if they waited for the hunters, but his people moved in the opposite direction from them. Laura's long blonde hair blew in the wind toward the buffalo, they thundered toward her. He jerked awake!

It was almost dawn. He was sore from the cold hard ground and shivered from the cold north wind whistling through the trees. His fire was almost out. It took him a while to bring the coals back to life and get warmth from the burning wood. He noticed Spotted Horse had moved closer to him during the night and had lain down nearby. It was unusual for him to do so and Talon wondered why.

Perhaps he sensed danger in the tall pines or a change in the weather or maybe both. Talon munched on roasted corn. Spotted Horse heard him eating the corn and rose to come over to him. He shared the corn with the horse knowing he would need the strength to get them home. They soon broke camp to continue their trek before the sun rose. All day Talon thought of his dream, wondering what it meant and how Laura played a part in it. He would talk with his mother when he got to their camp.

But as he approached the campsite there was no sign of his people. *What had happened to cause them to move? Where had they gone?* Worried, he searched the surrounding area for signs of the direction they had gone in. When he realized the tribe had divided itself, it caused him fear. It was something that should not have happened. *What could have caused it?*

Now he had to figure out which direction his mother and grand-father would have taken. The tribe had divided into three groups. One had gone to the south, another to the north, and the third to the east. He stood in the middle of the old campsite staring first in one direction then the other. He prayed to the Great Spirit to guide him to find his mother and he began walking in ever-widening circles crossing each route searching for the clue his mother would have left him.

As he got farther out, each trail was swept clean so they could not be followed. Finally, he spotted something. Kneeling by a bush, he found a small red-beaded fringe in his mother's special tribal pattern tied to the bottom of a bush. He knew what direction to go in to find her. When he reached them, they would tell him why the tribe had divided and he must tell her of his dream of buffalo and Laura. Perhaps she would be able to help him figure out what it meant.

CHAPTER 24

Four days of hard riding brought Talon upon the new campsite where his mother tended a pot over a tiny cooking fire. A crowd gathered, speaking over one another to share what had happened since he left. He needed to know. Chief Smoking Owl, his Grandfather, motioned for him to come into his tepee, so they could talk in private. His mother followed, closing the flap behind her.

"It took me four days of hard riding to find you. Why have you divided and moved in this direction?"

"My son, our people were frightened because there have been no buffalo," Smoking Owl said, sitting placidly upon a pile of furs. "They divided to search for food before the winter snows. We could not stop them once they thought of this plan. Your mother tried to convince them to stay together but they would not listen and they left. We chose this direction because there is a great rock shelter not far from here, but the game goes more scarce because of a lack of rain and the buffalo have not come. We are glad you are here. Have you had a vision?"

"I have had a strange vision, but I do not know what it means." He began relating the vision to them.

When he finished, his mother nodded. "And the Spirit Woman is somehow a part of this vision, too."

"Yes, our lives are intertwined, but it still is not clear to me how. Have you had any more visions of her, Mother?"

"She has been on the edges of my dreams as she is in yours. I have no meaning for them, but she is connected to us."

"She told me of a secret valley in the mountains and wants me to bring you there. There is a warm spring and it is sheltered from the snow. She has offered to share her small supply of food. And yes, Mother, she does speak with animals. She has asked if we come to promise not to harm the wolves who roam her mountains."

His mother and grandfather stared at him as they debated about what he had said. His mother asked, "Do you care for the Spirit Woman?"

He startled both of them saying, "She carries my child. I know I have charmed her as much as she has charmed me!"

After explaining to the remaining tribe members what had transpired, it was decided they would break camp at first light to begin the long trek to the hidden valley in the mountains of the Spirit Woman. As Talon lay wrapped in his buffalo robe that night, he thought of the last night he was with Laura. He grew hard remembering their long hours of loving and he longed for her. He relived the first time he watched Laura bathe in the spring and fell asleep dreaming of her.

The vision came again, but much more clearly this time. The buffalo were within reach. All he had to do was reach out to touch them. Laura was beckoning from the distant mountains with her long yellow hair waving in the breeze. He heard the roar and wondered if a storm was coming. The ground under his bed began to shudder and shake, as the rumbling grew louder.

A shout! He jerked awake as he realized what the noise was. A buffalo herd was thundering down on them.

"Grandfather! Mother! Get up! The buffalo are here!" He grabbed his bow and arrows and raced outside.

His cousins were outside their tepees watching as the buffalo raced a short distance away from their campsite. It was a small herd, but they were buffalo. The men were grinning at each other and praising the Great Spirit for saving them from starvation. They made plans to follow the herd but would wait until they settled down to graze. They leaped on their ponies riding for the herd. The excitement of the hunt clung to the warriors as they eased into the herd to shoot the ones they wanted. They needed to kill five or six. Their small group could not process more than that. If the main tribe had been together, they would have killed more, but now, they would do what they could.

By noon, they had killed six large males, enough to enjoy now and plenty to preserve for winter, dragging them close to camp for the women to begin skinning and cutting up the carcasses. Nothing went to waste; even the marrow in the bones was eaten after the bones were thrown in the fire to cook. It could then be mixed with jerky to form pemmican. The muscle meats were stripped, cut into strips and hung to dry in the sun to make into jerky. The hooves were used for glue and the stomachs for containers. The intestines were cooked and eaten or used to be containers for pemmican. The hides were rolled up and stored for later when they would have the time to work them into clothing or tepees. It took them five full days and nights to prepare the meat and hides.

Drying of the meat had begun immediately, so they could travel as soon as possible. Working rapidly, they watched the skies for the nearing winter. Late on the seventh day, Talon watched as the winds changed, bringing with it the scent of snow. The order was given to be ready to move at first light.

The traveling had been hard and fast for well over two weeks now trying to make it through the mountain passes before heavy snows closed them completely. As their trek drew them higher into the mountains, the snow became deeper and deeper. The People and their horses were exhausted as they neared the top of the canyon. They were able to retain their strength only because the Great Spirit had given them buffalo. Talon was anxious to return to Laura. He worried every day about her and her baby. *Was she all right? Did she need anything?* He couldn't get there quick enough.

Reaching the area Laura had told him to look for, Talon motioned for the People to wait while he scouted ahead to find the trail leading down into the lower canyon and the hidden valley. They were close. He could feel it. He had to find the entrance without falling off the cliff. As he moved around in the falling snow, he saw movement up ahead. A large silver wolf watched him as he searched for the trail. It turned, leading him to the break in the rocks and disappearing into it. It was Laura's wolf.

He followed the wolf tracks in the snow and into the rock opening, thankful it was wide enough for him to stand upright in the dark, cave-like, narrow corridor and wide enough for a horse to pass through. He entered a bright area filled with light revealing the hidden valley spread before him. Tall trees grew upward toward the deep cracks in the rock overhangs with roots and vines hanging downward to meet the trees. He could hear the gurgling of a spring somewhere nearby. There were plenty of places to erect tepees with room for the horses to graze. It was well protected from the winter winds and snow, but sunlight still filtered in from the top. It was a perfect place for the People. He thanked the Great Spirit for the safety of his People and for Laura. He turned to retrace his steps to begin bringing them down to safety.

Hours later, the last family member and their belongings came down the dangerous path and into the hidden valley. Old fallen trees, dry enough to burn, provided fuel and soon the old women had fires blazing to cook the evening meal for the People. Everyone was weary, and there was still much to do. Tonight though, they would eat and rest.

Tomorrow they would build a cover to hide the entrance to the valley from unwanted visitors. Tonight they would post guards to watch for any dangers. Talon wondered about the wolf he had followed. Looking around for him, he did not know how he managed to get out of the valley.

When he told his People not to harm the wolves, they'd agreed but were frightened of his woman who could talk with animals. Just as he had been until he knew her. Tomorrow he would go see how she had fared. It had been too long since he had been with her. He missed her greatly. He dreamed of their reunion.

A shout from the entrance brought all braves to their feet with drawn weapons as they rushed forward to meet the enemy. One lone man dressed in heavy furs entered their valley. He raised both hands and pulled his head covering back to reveal his face. It was Willow's husband, Two Horses. Everyone rushed forward except Willow's mother.

Talon reached him first. "Is all well with you, Two Horses?"

"We have been following you for many suns, unable to catch up because we could not travel fast enough," when he leaned on Talon trying to catch his breath.

"Who else is with you?" he asked.

"I need help getting Willow down here. She is heavy with child and is unable to go any further. Will you help us?"

Immediately, Talon's weariness was forgotten. He hurried through the narrow passage to begin the climb up the rock path toward Willow. He found her resting against a rock in a half sitting position. She had her hands on her big belly. "I am glad to see you, my brother. As you can see, I need your help."

He scooped her up, hugging her to him, while her husband and some of the others watched. Talon began the long and dangerous journey back down the narrow, rocky trail slowly, telling Willow to keep her head on his shoulder so he did not hit it on the rocks.

The only tepee erected was Chief Smoking Owl's. Running Fawn led the way as Talon carried Willow with Two Horses following. After getting Willow snuggled into warm furs, Running Fawn signaled Two Horses to sit down then served them fresh buffalo meat. The People had many questions but waited quietly until all had eaten.

"Two Horses has taken good care of my sister by bringing her to us, but what has happened to cause you to travel at a time like this with a baby coming?"

Two Horses gazed at the four faces as he sadly explained, "My tribe is in trouble. We have not been able to find food because of the dryness of the hunting grounds. We searched everywhere finding very little. We moved our camp many times during the warm summer days but still no buffalo. Many became ill. Many became frightened and discouraged."

Glancing at Willow with love in his eyes, he continued, "When we knew a baby would be coming, we decided to come to you for help. Willow lost a baby many moons ago. When we knew this one would be born, I decided she needed to be with her family who could help when the time came. Our tribe began to separate and our numbers grew smaller. Willow and I prayed to the Great Spirit to lead us to her family. She had a vision of a place of safety in these mountains. As we traveled the mountain trail, we discovered others traveled before us. There were signs it was Willow's people. We are relieved to have found you when we did."

Smoking Owl grinned at Two Horses. "We are happy you are here with us. Our tribe has divided also, and we are few in numbers. Perhaps we will survive the winter because of the Spirit Woman."

"Who is this Spirit Woman?" Two Horses asked.

No one spoke until Running Fawn said, "Talon's woman. She has been in our visions and dreams for some time. She has led us here to this hidden valley for the winter. She asks one thing of us. We must not kill the wolves. They are hers. She talks to animals and they to her."

Willow gasped.

"Willow, do you know of this woman?" her mother asked loudly.

"Talon," she asked. "What does your Spirit Woman look like?"

Talon watched Willow's expressions as he began to describe Laura.

"Does she have a name or is she Spirit Woman?" Willow asked.

"Her name is Laura."

Willow gasped again.

"Daughter, do you know this woman?" demanded her mother.

"She saved me from a bear when I was hunting herbs for your medicines and tonics nearby. My leg was trapped, and I could not move. The bear came at me but Laura shot an ear off and her silver wolf chased the bear away. We became great friends. We taught each other about healing plants and how to use them. When I was to marry Two Horses, she told me the same thing had happened to her and she had been forced to wed an old man. She reminded me Two Horses probably did not want to marry me either. He was forced by his tribe, also." She glanced at Two Horses. "She told me to be the best wife I could be and make him love me. She said I would be happy and so would my new husband, and she was right. We do love each other now, but in the beginning, we did not. She had wise advice and I have thought of her many times since I have been gone. I thought I recognized the area when we came up here, but with the snow, I could not be sure."

Talon was pleased to know Laura had contact with his family even before he knew her. She was amazing, his Spirit Woman.

Pulling a small gold chain with a heart shaped locket from around her neck, she said, "The last time we saw each other, she gave me this locket. It was something special to her. When can I see her?"

"That may not be as easy as you think," replied Talon. "You are big with child and unable to move fast. Laura carries my child as well." There were loud gasps at his surprising news.

"You have gotten my friend with child. How could you?" yelled Willow.

Talon and the rest laughed loudly at Willow's indignation of her brother's activities with her friend.

"I will leave at first light tomorrow. She needs my protection." He beamed at Willow.

CHAPTER 25

Many long and lonesome weeks had passed since Talon's departure. Laura missed him every day and especially at night. She continued to do her chores, ever mindful of her expanding waistline and the increasing bad weather. The days continued to grow colder, the skies heavy with the promise of more snow. Talon would return to her as soon as he could, but it did not keep her from worrying about him.

Five days before, a blizzard blew in dumping a great deal of snow, but no more followed. Each day she managed to wade through a foot of snow to the barn to feed the animals. After her trip to the barn this morning, she worked in the cabin making candles and then sewing baby clothes.

She felt tired as she added potatoes, carrots, and onions to the pot of stew she prepared for supper. Earlier she had started melting snow for her bath. Slipping out of her robe, she stepped into the heated water in the tub.

A loud sigh of contentment escaped her lips as she settled back. The warmth soothed the aches in her back and legs caused by her pregnancy. She stared at the flames in the fireplace, reflecting on how she came to be with child. Her memories were still vivid and she hugged her rounding belly and thought, *One of you wonderful angel men gave me a special gift. I will treasure it always.* She shook herself out of her reverie and began to lather up the scented soap purchased in Denver. She loved the smell of the soap and her rose creams and lotions as well. When the water began to cool, she stepped out of the tub. Standing naked before the fireplace, she dried her pregnant body.

A strange noise on the porch drew her attention. Was it the wind or was something on the porch? Slipping into her robe, she drew it about her swollen body and eased toward her rifle.

A muffled knock startled her. A sound like her name penetrated her fear. "Who's there?" she called. Again, a muffled knock and her name.

She unbolted the heavy door allowing Talon to enter covered in snowy buckskins and fur. Dropping the backpack, he removed the snow-covered coat. She hung it on a hook, then helped him out of the snowshoes and knee-high leggings.

She stripped him naked, then wrapped him in a quilt and led him to the fireplace. Concerned about frostbite to his toes and feet, she pushed him into one of the rocking chairs and fetched a basin of cool water for him to put his feet into.

Slowly she began to add warm water from a kettle heating on the stove. He groaned and she massaged his feet with a warmed towel to restore circulation in them.

"I have missed you, my Spirit Woman," he said with both hands wrapped around a mug of hot tea. "You have grown quite large since I have been gone."

"You have been gone for many weeks. I feared you wouldn't return. Were you able to find the valley and get your people safely there?" she asked.

"Yes. We found buffalo, which delayed us from coming sooner, but we have meat for the winter. When I found the tribe, they had split into three groups. I have brought my mother's family here. We sent scouts to look for the others, but they have vanished. We have asked the Great Spirit to protect them. The weather turned bad and we had to begin the trek into the mountains. My sister and her husband found us as well, so my family has been reunited. What were you doing before I came?" he asked as he noticed the large copper bathtub near the fireplace.

"I'd just finished bathing. I ached in my bones from the cold, so I decided a nice warm bath would be wonderful, and it was," she grinned at him lustily.

He opened his arms inviting her to sit on his lap in the rocking chair. She rushed into them with a cry. "I've missed you so much! I'm glad you are here. Please hold me tight and never let me go." She buried her face against his neck.

After a while, he opened her robe. Her breasts had enlarged and her large protruding stomach pushed against him. The look on his face told Laura he noticed all the changes taking place in her body since he had last seen her naked. She tried to jerk the robe closed.

He grabbed her hands, saying lovingly, "I had not expected you to become so large. You are beautiful," as he rose from the chair pulling her against his nakedness. However, her large, rounded stomach prevented him from holding her close.

"I'm too large now to make love," she cried with tears in her eyes.

He looked down at her, "Spirit Woman, there are different ways to love a woman when she is great with child. If you are willing, we will try them."

"Would you like to bathe in the tub? I promise you'll enjoy it if I help you," she said with a twinkle in her eyes.

And, he did.

In the early morning light, Laura stretched like a feline. She remembered the night with Talon in her bed. He had been gentle but passionate. Such pleasure they had shared. She turned to look at him in sleep. He seemed to be content and it pleased her.

She slipped out of bed to prepare the morning coffee. As she did so, Talon opened his eyes as the corn shuck filled mattress made noises when she rose. He watched her from the bed as she moved slowly about preparing the coffee.

"I have something for you from my mother," he said as he rose to go to his backpack still on the floor by the door. Retrieving it, he handed her a gift from his mother wrapped in soft deerskin.

"From your mother?" she asked pleased to know she had sent her a gift. He nodded.

Laura pulled back the deerskin covering to discover a large necklace made from bear claws. "These are from the bear you killed. My mother fashioned a necklace for you. I gave her small gold nuggets and turquoise stones to go with the claws. The bear hunter is honored with her talisman of courage," he explained as he placed the necklace over her head and around her neck. She was speechless. He kissed her tenderly.

He gave her a large bundle of dried leaves tied with rawhide as well. She turned it this way and that, trying to figure out what it could be. "What is it?"

"This is Scared Sage and it is used to ward off evil spirits from your home and family. It is a gift from my sister, Willow, to her friend, Laura," he said with a gleam in his eyes.

Laura gasped. "Willow is your sister? How is she? Where is she? Please tell me everything about her. I've worried so much about her. When can we go see her?" she spoke the questions in rapid fire.

He pulled her to him, telling her everything he knew about what had happened to Willow.

~

Now the weeks seemed endless. There were days they were able to leave the cabin, but Laura had to be careful of icy spots. She never ventured far. Talon cared for the livestock. His actions were so funny as she taught him to milk the cow. He told Laura it was beneath a warrior's dignity to do so, but he did it for her. She had figured out how to carefully handle the cow, but was glad to let Talon do it. His love of butter and honey on his hot biscuits outweighed his warrior's pride.

One clear day, he left early to travel to the hidden valley, taking with him as much milk and butter as he could carry. He returned exhausted by nightfall, reporting all was well with his family and that Willow was even larger than Laura. Laura hoped Willow was not that large, because she was becoming more miserable as the weeks went by.

When Christmas Eve came, Laura asked Talon if he would cut down a small spruce tree and bring it into the cabin. She sensed he thought her request strange, but did as she asked him. She placed the tree on a small table and began to decorate it with colored paper and hand painted ornaments she took from a large chest. She explained she always put up a tree to acknowledge Christ's birthday even though she did not have any presents to put under it. She told him about Christ and the Bible, which was as important to her as his belief in the Great Spirit was to him. They talked about their strong faiths and drew closer because of the sharing and understanding.

During this time, he taught her more about the herbs she had drying on the corner shelf. He showed her how to mix them for better effectiveness when treating illnesses. They learned from each other ways to treat various ailments.

Talon showed her often how much he cared for her. She began to learn to trust again. However, when he talked of her becoming his wife, she would withdraw from him. She had a fear she could not bring to the surface about being controlled again by a man. Time would tell if she changed her mind. Although she loved him with all of her heart, she would not marry him.

CHAPTER 26

When the New Year dawned on a windy and snowy morning, Laura rose from her bed with a happy heart. Her child would be born in a few weeks, and then her life would change forever. She would become a mother, she thought to herself, as she went to start a pot of coffee. When she bent over to stoke the coals and add more wood in the cook stove, a sharp pain sliced up her middle. She grasped and moaned. Talon was out of bed and by her side. "Is the baby coming?" he asked fearfully.

"I'm not sure. Let me finish preparing the coffee and we will wait to see what happens next," she said, trying to sound brave for him. However, as she placed the coffee pot on the stove to boil, another pain more intense than the first shot through her. She felt a wetness running down her legs, soaking into her socks and house shoes. Bloody tinged water ran out and onto the floor. Fearfully she said to Talon, "Yes, the baby is coming and coming quickly I think. Now what do we do?"

"You are asking me? I have never had a child before either. Come sit down. No, maybe you should lie down. Or should you walk? I have seen Indian women walking around the campsite before their children were born."

Another stabbing pain gripped her as she stood there. She had not recovered from that one before another came. She had not expected the pains to hurt so bad and to come so fast. "I think something might be wrong."

"I will go for my mother, but you must lie down while I am gone. I do not want you to fall." He spread blankets and sheets onto the bed and helped her lie down. He placed drinking water near the bed and several cloths for her to wipe her face.

Dressed in his winter gear to begin the long trek to get his mother, he kissed her goodbye as he hurried to the door. Putting on his snowshoes, he latched the door and left the cabin sprinting.

The level of pain continued to intensify. She could no longer control her screams. She heard a wolf howl. Silver had come to let her know she was not alone. At least she felt a little comfort. Then another pain grabbed her and she cried out again. Deciding she needed a cup of soothing hot tea, she willed herself to roll over on her side so she could push up.

When she managed to rise from the bed, she hurried to the stove to put the kettle on. Another ripping contraction assailed her.

After preparing the tea, she struggled back to bed. She drank the tea and lay back down. The contractions were becoming never ending. She wiped her face with a cool cloth and used it to muffle her cries. Time seem to stand still. She was locked in unending agony.

Reality faded for Laura as her mind filled with nothing but the hurt. *Why did it have to be this way? Why do I always have to be alone? Why? Why? Why?*

A cold cloth bathed her face, and soothing words of comfort were whispered to her. She was no longer alone. She must be dying. She knew nothing but ripping and pulling. She was dying and God had sent another angel to help her to Heaven.

"What? What are you saying?" she whispered. *Is someone speaking to me?*

She was lifted up and a cup held to her lips. She sputtered, as she tasted the bitter drink. *"Why does it always have to be bitter herbs?"* she thought. Or did she say it?

"What? Open my eyes? Hurts too badly. Can't open eyes," she whispered.

"Yes, you can Laura. Open your eyes and look at me." The voice was louder this time.

Laura looked into the scarred face of a dark stranger. No wait. It was the face of...the face of...."I know you from the trading post when Tuffy attacked me, but not your name."

"Call me Marty. I heard you crying and I'm here to help. Will you trust me?" Marty asked her.

"Yes. You helped me once before. I know you won't hurt me. But do you know anything about birthing babies?" she asked.

Marty assured her. "I know all there is to know. Will you trust me, Laura?"

Laura nodded, sucking in a breath.

"Let me help you up. I want you to walk and breathe in deeply. It is good for you as well as for the baby. Do you understand?"

Not waiting for Laura to answer, Marty pulled her up to a standing position and walked her up and down the width of the cabin.

A wolf howled.

"Why is a wolf howling outside your door?" Marty asked nervously.

"Oh, it's Silver. He's my protector and he doesn't like it when I scream. Please don't be afraid. He won't hurt you unless you hurt me."

"I will stay inside as long as he is near."

After a few more trips back and forth, Laura's legs would not hold her up, though her pains did become less intense as she walked. "I feel something wet between my legs," Laura cried.

"It may be the baby's head. Lie down on the bed and let me see," Marty ordered.

"I will not. I will not allow you to see my private parts. You're a man!" Laura declared.

Marty stepped back smiling. "It seems to me a man got you in this shape. And you are refusing my help because I'm a man?"

"Sounds pretty stupid at a time like this, doesn't it? Alright. What do you want me to do?"

"Lie back down on the bed and let me see if the baby's head is pushing out."

Marty helped her to lie down and peered between her legs. "Well, I don't see the head yet so it will take more time. I have birthed Indian women before, and they have a unique way of making it less painful. At least it's what I've heard. Are you game to try?"

"Anything to make it easier."

Helping her to rise again from the bed and taking her hand, Marty led her over before the fireplace and placed a quilt on the floor. "Now get down on your knees and prop your head and your arms on this chair seat. When you feel one starting, begin to rock back and forth on your knees."

Laura managed to get on her knees with Marty's help as another series of contractions began. As each one ended, another stronger one took its place. Marty fixed her another cup of soothing tea.

As Laura drank the tea, Marty knelt down beside her. "I want to check on your progress. May I feel to see where the baby has moved to?" Laura nodded. "Indian women tell me Mother Earth helps them pull the baby from their bodies in this position. Can you feel the difference? Lying in bed made you feel more pain and you had to work harder. This way you are more comfortable and working with the pains instead of against them."

"My back already feels better since I am not lying on it." She tensed. "Something is moving!"

"Yes, yes, it is working already. Soon you will be a mother!"

"Well, well, if this isn't a cozy picture!" said a hate-filled voice from the doorway.

Startled at the sound of an unexpected voice, Marty and Laura looked up to see Tuffy Sawyer standing inside the cabin door, pointing a long-barreled pistol at both of them. His mouth widened in a toothless grin.

Laura screamed. The monster was in her cabin and she was helpless to do anything about it. Her growing concern now was for the safety of her baby.

Marty straightened up beside Laura, towering over Tuffy.

"What did you do with that squaw whore you stole from me?" Tuffy demanded.

"Aponi was not a whore. But she was captured by a son of a whore who starved and beat her," Marty replied with hatred.

"The whore had a name, did she? Well, I am sure you enjoyed her as much as I did."

"Aponi means Butterfly. After I rescued her from you, I took her back to her people to die. She is now a free spirit and a true butterfly."

"She's dead? Another good Indian."

"Before she died, she became ill from a disease she had gotten from you or other palefaces," Marty said enjoying the look of terror that took over Tuffy's face. "I do not know the name, but the symptoms are not very pretty."

"Symptoms? What kind of symptoms?" waving his gun nervously at Marty.

"First it burns to pee and then large sores appear on your manhood and other places. Then yellow stinking puss oozes out of your cock before it rots off."

Tuffy grabbed his crotch.

When his attention changed, Marty flew through the air and brought them both crashing to the floor. Marty may have been taller, but Tuffy was strong and solid. They rolled and tumbled about the cabin knocking over furniture as they struggled over the gun.

The loud explosion of the pistol brought everything to a halt. Laura screamed in fear when Tuffy rose from the melee.

"You killed him!" Laura whimpered.

"So you and your mulatto lover are having a baby. Isn't that interesting?" Tuffy came toward her with blood splatter on his face and clothes.

He grabbed her hair dragging her upward to face him. She screamed in terror and fear. He slapped her hard across the face as he released her. She hit the floor and struck her head.

~

Swirls of haze circled before her eyes. Realizing she was swimming up to consciousness, she tried to open her eyes to see where Tuffy was. He had

168

tied her spread eagle on the bed. Another searing pain tore at her as the baby tried to push out, but now she tried to keep him in to protect him.

Tuffy stood over her.

"You can't get loose now, you whoring bitch. I am going to slice you open and let you see what you created with that mulatto before you die. If the baby lives, I will raise it to be just like me, or pimp it out if it's a girl," he enjoyed seeing the terror he created with his words.

"Why do you hate me so? What have I ever done to you?" Laura managed to get out.

"You ruined my business when you came in flirting and wiggling your ass around making me want to mount you. The word spread about what happened with you and Abner, and folks quit coming in. Then when you brought in those nuggets, I paid you with money I had stashed. Someone followed me and discovered all the places I had my money buried. They stole it. I know it was you!"

"But I didn't do any of that to you. You want to blame me for your troubles. How did you find me?" She bit her lip to keep from screaming, she tasted blood.

"When I had you tailed, the trail was always lost in this area. I came searching, watching for smoke or the smell of wood burning. When I smelled it, I followed it into this valley. I knew I'd found the right place when I heard you screaming your head off."

"But I didn't do anything to you," whimpered Laura as another pain tore through her.

"I'm not going to argue with you about it. I know you did it," He cut her bloody nightgown from top to bottom revealing her nakedness. After a few moments, he drew the sharp tip of his skinning knife across her belly as if he was preparing to cut a watermelon. He nicked her in places, causing blood to ooze out and slide down her sides soaking the bed. Laura screamed in terror and agony.

"Tuffy, I beg you. Please don't do this. You may hurt my baby," she whimpered.

He grinned.

"Milford Crouch, what do you think you are doing to that woman?" Tuffy's knife froze in midair as he heard a voice say his birth name.

Behind him, Marty held a gun pointed at Tuffy's heart. Blood dripped from a mangled face, flowing down his cheek and neck.

"How do you know me, friend?" Tuffy asked.

"I've told you before, I'm not your friend. I am a ghost from your sorry past, you son of a whore. You don't remember me do you? Perhaps this will remind you." He pulled long black hair from the bloodied left side of his face.

A jagged scar ran along the man's left cheekbone and into the hairline.

"Well, well, well, Martha Lane. You bitch! I thought I killed you long ago in that fire. Now I get the chance to do it right this time."

"The fire. Yes, I nearly died after you hit me in the head with a steel rod and left me in that burning building. But you also got burned, judging from the scars on your scalp. Shame you didn't die in the fire as well. I have something for you. I think you'll remember how this works," Marty pulled a small doll out of her pocket.

Tuffy gasped, "A voodoo doll."

"When I knocked you out in the trading post, I cut off some of your hair for the doll and I took one of your dirty shirts to make it some clothes. Don't you think the gris-gris looks like you?" Marty removed a long straight pin and began chanting in French.

"You damn voodoo queen! I tried to kill you in New Orleans and it didn't happen. But now I'll make sure you're dead." He lunged for her, but she sidestepped.

Taking the pin, she plunged it into the left thigh of the small doll. He plunged his knife into his left leg and shrieked. Pulling the pin out again, she plunged it into the left arm of the doll. He jabbed the knife into his left arm, then jerked his hand away. The blade clattered to the floor.

Laura watched the events unfolding and was relieved when the knife dropped to the floor.

When Marty plunged the pin into the doll's stomach, he bent over and grabbed his middle. As she pushed the pin between the doll's legs, Tuffy screamed, clutching his crotch as he dropped to the floor.

"I can keep doing this all day and enjoy every minute of it."

"Please stop! Let me leave and you'll never see me again," he pleaded.

"If I had not stopped you, you would've hurt Laura and her baby, so why should I let you go?" Marty's tone was deadly.

"I'm sorry if I scared you, Laura. Just let me go and you'll never hear from me again. I promise," whined Tuffy.

"Get up and get out. We have a baby to bring into this world," Marty said pleasantly.

"Please no more pins and dolls. I'm going," he whimpered scrambling for his hat and coat. A box of matches fell from his pocket as he fled. *Had he planned to burn down the cabin?*

She was quick to bolt the door to prevent him from returning.

Marty returned to the bed and freed Laura. She examined the wounds on her belly and assured her they were minor.

Laura writhed in the next contraction. "Will this never end?" she screamed.

Marty checked her progress. "It won't be long now. I already see more of the head than before. When you feel the pressure, bear down and push," Marty told her.

Please let Talon return soon.

From outside, a long wolf howl ended in a human scream, but she had no time for worrying about Tuffy coming to a bad end. The bastard had tried to kill her and the baby. Let Silver punish him for his crimes.

CHAPTER 27

Eagle Talon had not realized the snow was as deep as it was when he left Laura. It was taking him longer to reach his Mother than he had expected. Suddenly, a fast-traveling party of two on snowshoes came into view. Talon recognized his mother's winter coat and shouted her name. Two Horses raised his spear at Talon then waved.

"I was coming for you, Mother. Laura is in hard labor and she needs help." He stepped back. "But why are you here?"

"My son, I had a vision last night. I knew I needed to be here with you and Laura. She is in trouble. We must hurry." She headed down the path and the two men fell in behind her.

Talon heard Laura's screams before they saw the cabin. He sped up and arrived on the porch ahead of the others. Wolf tracks covered the porch and marred the snow as if one had been pacing around.

When they tried to enter the cabin, the door was bolted. Talon pounded on the heavy wood and the door swung open to reveal a tall dark, menacing stranger with a knife in his hand.

Before Talon could react, the stranger said, "Are you Talon? Laura has been calling for you. Please come here."

"You're here," Laura called out. "Hurry, your son is about to be born."

Kneeling by her side, Talon wiped her red sweating face with a damp cloth. "I am here, my Spirit Woman, and have brought my mother, Running Fawn."

All she could do was nod at his mother. She felt soothing hands as she was touched and repositioned. A wet cloth wiped the sweat from her brow and tears from her eyes. She focused on Talon's face above her and strained to make sense of his words through the haze of pain.

"Mother is here to help you," he said. "She was already on her way."

"Laura, I am Running Fawn, Talon and Willow's mother."

"Thank you for coming, Running Fawn. Yes, I need your help. This is Marty, my friend. She will help too," Laura, breathed hard between each word.

Running Fawn bent Laura's knees and spread her legs to be able to see how far she had progressed.

"Laura, I must wash my hands before I can help you. I will hurry."

Running Fawn returned to her side and gave her an encouraging smile. "Now push down with all your might!"

Laura gripped Talon's hand, and felt the baby slip from her body. Immediately, she felt great relief.

Running Fawn pulled the infant from the watery flood, opened the sack to remove the baby, and laid it upon its mother's belly. Talon saw its sex and said, "Laura, it's a son!" Laura beamed, but in the next breath, she gripped his hand when another searing, cutting contraction surprised her.

"Bear down hard again, Laura, we have another baby coming!" Running Fawn exclaimed as she helped a blond-haired baby make its appearance into the world. She laid it next to the other on Laura's belly as everyone stared at the contrast between the two. The first boy was dark with black hair and the second baby boy had fair skin with light-colored hair. The silence was deafening.

Fearfully Laura asked, "Are they both all right? I think they are early. Will they live?"

Running Fawn had been busy tying off each baby's cord with rawhide. She handed Talon the knife, asking if he wanted to cut the cords on the babies, making them his. He grabbed the knife and cut where she indicated. They wrapped the babies in butter-soft buckskin blankets that Running Fawn had brought with her, and snuggled them next to their mother.

Running Fawn began to massage Laura's belly and before long, she expelled the afterbirths of both babies. They were not identical twins because they did not come out of the same sac. She knew they did not belong to her son by their looks, but if he wanted to claim them, she would keep silent.

The babies began squirming and nudging at their mother's breasts for food. Running Fawn taught Laura how to feed her new babies. "Your milk will not come in for a few days, but the babies need the beginnings in your breasts to help keep them healthy." Before long, Laura and the two babies were cleaned and put to bed. In a short time, the three were asleep.

Two crying hungry babies soon woke up wanting attention. Laura was hungry as well since she had not eaten since the night before. She had many questions and few answers about the turn of events, beginning with Marty.

Running Fawn had sewed the jagged edges of Marty's wound together with her tiny stitches. "I think the wound will heal now and not leave an ugly scar."

"Thank you, Running Fawn," Marty said. "When I was injured before, I had no one to care for me and it healed by itself."

"Marty, you appear to be a man, but you are a woman," Laura said. "Why? And how did you know I would need your help again? How did you find my cabin?"

"You are full of questions," Marty chuckled. "It's a long story. Do you want the long or the short of it?"

"I want to know all about you. You saved my life twice and I don't know why."

"I was born a slave to a black mother and a white father. My father was the master of the plantation and had say over everyone's destiny. He became angry with my mother one day and sold me to a man in New Orleans who liked little girls. This man raped me many times before I was able to escape. The witchdoctors in New Orleans took me in because I had special talents. They taught me how to use my powers. After I became stronger in my knowledge, no one dared return me to my master. Those witchdoctors dealt in voodoo."

"What is voodoo?" Laura asked.

"It is a powerful assembly who work with spirits. Mostly for good, but some can be evil spirits. I was in training to be a voodoo queen when I grew older, but it wasn't what I wanted to do. I grew tired of New Orleans and my place. Because I was mulatto, I had a position in society, which I could not move out of. I wanted to be able to live my life as I chose to...not as someone else determined.

"When I was almost killed by that evil man who was here tonight, I knew I couldn't stay there, so when I had healed, I stole men's clothes and got a job on a riverboat up the Mississippi River. As time went on, I heard about gold strikes in Colorado, and decided to try my luck. It was safer for me to live and travel if I looked like a man. I'm pretty good at it, too. Most of the time people think I am." Marty struck a match and lit a black cigar puffing on it and creating smoke rings.

"The day at the trading post when I protected Laura from Tuffy raping her, I discovered who he was. I knew I would kill him but wanted it to be in a special way. I followed Laura when she managed to steal her horses back and come home. That's how I knew where to find you. Several weeks ago, I began having visions of Laura in need of my help. In the lurking shadows of my dreams, I sensed an evil being, but couldn't be sure who it was. But my visions urged me to come quickly."

"I am going after this evil man who tried to take my world from me," Talon jerked on his coat.

Marty shook her head, "It's not necessary, Talon. It has been taken care of. He will not ever harm Laura again."

"How do you know?" He continued to gather his winter gear to leave.

"The wolf Laura calls Silver, her protector, took care of the evil that harmed both of us. It's not a good idea to go out tonight, though. There is still danger in the forest." Her voice held a tone of warning.

Talon stopped. "Thank you for helping Laura. You are right to stop me."

Running Fawn laid a hand on her son's arm. "The vision that started me here also showed an evil presence overshadowing Laura and her two babies."

"So you knew before you got here she would deliver two and didn't tell me?" Talon asked.

"Yes, I knew. Your sister delivered two boy babies several suns ago." She looked at the beaming father, Two Horses. "We have received four babies for me to help care for."

~

After the twins were born, Laura and Talon asked Marty to stay on the ranch to live and work for them. Marty was pleased to stay because, as she told Laura, she had a few surprises of her own. She figured she was about three months pregnant. So her baby would be born about May or June.

"But how can you be expecting a baby?" Laura asked.

"Really, Laura? You of all people should ask me that?"

"I mean...how...when...who?"

"I will answer who. When I returned Aponi to her family in the Dakotas, I saw a handsome brave. Of course, I looked like a man and didn't think he even noticed me. Later, I went for a moonlight swim and he joined me. I was courted and loved as I have never been in my life. I fell for him. And even as big as I am, he fell for me. My life was happy for the first time. Late last fall, the braves were on a hunting trip and encountered a troop of soldiers, who fired on them. He was killed. I thought my life was over. When his tribe started to move to winter grounds, they didn't want me to go with them because I had no brave to hunt for me. I had visions about you being in danger, but I needed your help as well."

"Then you will stay with us," Laura said as she hugged Marty. "As soon as the winter is over, I'll have cabins built for you and for another couple who will be coming up from Denver to work for me. For now, we will fix you a bed here in the cabin, and you will be snug as a bug in a rug."

"Who is the other couple?" asked Marty, suddenly having a strange sensation.

"I met them last summer when I visited in Denver. They are John and Sadie Long. He'll work on the ranch with the horses and she'll help with cooking and chores. She has twin girls and knows all about taking care of twins." Noticing an excited look on Marty's face, Laura asked, "What's the matter, Marty? Are you not well? Is it the baby?"

"I had a sister named Sadie, but we were separated when I was sold."

"Oh my goodness! I heard your name but I've just now realized you are Sadie's long lost sister!" Laura waited breathlessly for her answer.

Laura studied her features and skin coloring. "I never noticed before because of your hair and clothes, but you do look like Sadie."

"You are an amazing woman, Laura. From the first time I saw you, there has been an aura about you drawing me to you. You have managed to save your ranch for your children. And now you tell me Sadie and I may finally be reunited."

"I pray it will all come together for you and your sister. She is a wonderful person and has gifts like you do."

The winter was bitter, but Laura had wisely prepared her family and Talon's tribe for it. His tribe thrived with the buffalo meat and fresh kills of deer and elk. The hunters did not have to go far to find game. When the warm winds began to blow, melting the snow, Laura's spirits rose. The winter would soon be over. When the passes were opened, she sent for carpenters to begin building the cabins needed for Marty and the Longs.

Marty was anxious to surprise her sister. The days dragged by. But finally, the cabins were completed and Laura sent for the Longs.

～

When their wagon pulled up to Laura's cabin, John helped Sadie and the twins down. Laura rushed into Sadie's arms giving her a big hug, "My dear friend, it's been too long."

Sadie wiped tears from her eyes as she returned the hug, "I have missed you and counted the days until we could come here. Your ranch is beautiful."

"Thank you, Sadie."

Laura then embraced the twins and slipped them each a piece of candy from her pocket. "I have a special surprise for you, Sadie. Please look at the cabin door."

Sadie looked up as Marty walks onto the porch. Screaming loudly, Sadie ran up the steps with her arms opened wide grabbing her long lost sister in a tight embrace.

Amid many tears and much laughter, the sisters didn't let go of each other. Calling John and the twins over, Sadie introduced her family to Marty.

"We have much to talk about, big sister," Sadie said to Marty, as she patted her rounding belly.

"Yes, we do. But for now, I want to show you to your new cabin, which is next door to mine."

Laura stood back, observing the happy reunion. She was happier than she had ever been in her young life. She knew now that in order to receive love, you have to be able to give your love to others.

EPILOGUE

May, 1888 Spotted Horse Ranch

Laura sat at her dining table in her quiet cabin, lost in memories. How quickly time had passed. She knew from the moment the twins were born, who their fathers were. She had written their names in her Bible as James William McKenna Brown and Samuel Eli Adams Brown. She called them Will and Eli Brown so her sons would never know the label of bastard because of what their mother had done. No one would ever know the truth while she was alive.

She had finally, agreed to marry Talon in a Ute Indian ceremony because before she had the twins weaned, she was pregnant again. Talon's mother made Laura a multi-colored beaded, white doeskin fringed wedding dress with lace up sides for an expanding waistline. For Talon, she sewed a white buckskin fringed vest with matching fringed pants in the same beaded designs as Laura's dress. Five months after the ceremony, Black Hawk was born. Black Hawk looked exactly like his father. Laura added his name in her Bible as well. Calling him, Levi, after her father. His full name was Levi Black Hawk Ralston.

A year later, their precious daughter, Laura Raven Ralston, was born. She had the European features of Talon's French father. When Running Fawn held her, she saw the likeness to Talon's father, a French trapper, and cried. With olive skin and black hair that gleamed in the sunlight like a raven's wing, she was beautiful. Laura's world had been made complete.

After Raven's birth, Laura made sure she drank a special tea that prevented any more children. Talon could not figure out why she never conceived again, even though he was always ready to warm the furs with her.

Laura refused to give up the Spotted Horse Ranch to live in an Indian village as a squaw. In early spring, after the twins were born, Laura's six brood mares foaled with spotted colts from Spotted Horse, Talon's stud. She remembered the shock of seeing a sea of white spotted foals. God had blessed her with her wonderful family, her loves, and awesome events in her life.

Talon refused to live on a horse ranch in a cabin and be a rancher, so after a few years of arguing, they compromised. She lived in her cabin on Widow's Peak, raising spotted horses, and he divided his time between his people and his family. They moved his tepee closer to her cabin so they could have their privacy when Talon came to visit.

Oh, those were glorious days and nights when they went to warm the furs in his tepee. Sometimes, they visited the forest. Chasing each other naked among the trees and making beautiful love on the ground among the leaves. They were happy as they raised their children in both worlds.

The children learned the Indian ways as well as the white man's ways. They learned to read and write and to read signs and hunt for food. When they were older, they could choose their own paths.

She bought any land adjoining her ranch when it became available. As time passed, the ranch became quite large. She liked the isolation because as white settlers moved into the area and learned of her Indian husband and half-breed children, they did not want anything to do with them.

The wars with the Indians caused many worries and concerns for her family. Laura wanted to remove her children from any kind of prejudice. The ranch was self-sustaining, so she made sure her family did not need anything from anyone. She had created a market for her spotted horses, selling to people who could afford them and care for them and not to locals who would use them as plow horses.

After a few years, Laura knew the one-room cabin was too small for her growing family. She had a large ranch house built and added more cabins behind the big house for her expanding employees, a bunkhouse for ranch hands, and a new larger horse barn. Sadie and John already lived in one of the first two cabins she had built, and Marty and her son lived in the other.

She hired carpenters from Denver who worked for almost a year constructing all the buildings she wanted. She went to Denver a number of times, purchasing furnishings for the ranch house, wanting to make it as modern as she could.

While in Denver on one occasion, she hired a famous painter to come to the ranch to paint her and Talon's portrait. Talon refused to pose for the painting at first. However, after refusing to sleep with him for several nights, he came around and allowed himself to be painted.

After the painting was finished, he was proud of it because it showed everyone Laura was his. She wore a blue silk ball gown with her bear claw necklace as her only jewelry. His muscular brazened chest was bare except for his eagle claw necklace, his beaded white-fringed buckskin leggings and beaded moccasins. His right arm was around her waist in a possessive manner. Their great love could be seen reflected in the painting. The painting now hung in the family room over the massive fireplace in the lodge.

Remembering the move into the house always brought tears to her eyes because at the last minute she could not leave her precious cabin with all of its memories. Her children were angry with her because she moved them there and stayed behind. After a while, the tension eased with them and everything returned to normal. She would always be there when the children rose and came downstairs each morning. She cooked their breakfast, and taught them their lessons.

However, when the night shadows began to fall, she would kiss them good night and walk back to her cabin that contained all her wonderful memories. She and Talon had been able to resume their nights of wild and noisy lovemaking without having to remind each other not to wake the children. Life in her valley continued happy and peaceful.

Their children grew strong and happy. They knew their parents loved them and shared a great love for each other. They grew up in two worlds, happy with their way of life.

Laura's eyes misted when she remembered past years. The older sons were now becoming adults. Most of the elders in their lives had passed away, but one strong force that remained was their Ute grandmother, Running Fawn. She was always there to teach and instruct them. They knew old ones and young ones who became ill and died, or had terrible accidents and died. Death happened to other people, never to them.

Tears flowed down Laura's cheeks as she remembered the horrible day their world had been shattered. Talon was killed hunting buffalo with his tribe. As she and the children lived through the Ute ritual of burying their dead, they could not believe he was gone. What would they do without him? What would she do without him?

Laura had asked herself that question many times since his death. The spark had disappeared from her life. She had always been full of life but ever since she lost Talon, a great sadness had come over her. She began to allow Will and Eli to take over most of her chores as she spent more time sitting in her rocking chair puffing on her pipe and reading her Bible or sitting on her bench on the "Widow's Peak" looking out over her valley. Life without her love had become dark.

Laura sighed as she finished writing in her journal. She stared at the final date she entered. She could not believe so much time had passed. Yet, it seemed so short because she had always stayed busy. Thinking back over the highs and lows of her life, she could not believe it had all happened to her.

She had forgiven Abner long ago for bringing her to such a remote place and deserting her, but never for his abuse of her. She had fought for survival, and had become stronger for it. She raised four wonderful children and had the love of a great man, who she missed every day. She prayed she had taught her children to be strong, trustworthy, and honest people.

She struggled with Will and Eli, forming them into the men they should be. She did not want them to take life for granted, but to know they could accomplish much by working hard and living righteously. When she was gone, they would discover how wealthy they were. She never told them about the gold nuggets and the bank in Denver, but they would soon find out. What would they do? How would they conduct themselves? She pondered about them.

She wondered what lifestyle Black Hawk would choose for himself, the Indian ways or the white man's ways. Always the quiet one like his father, she never knew what he was thinking. His love for both his families ran deep, and he was torn between the two. The terrible Indian wars caused trouble and concern for all those she loved. He would have to make his path the best way he could. She prayed she and Talon had taught him to choose wisely.

Her beautiful daughter, Raven, was sent away to Laura's sister Jane in Washington two years ago. She prayed every day Raven would settle in and learn the things her aunt could teach her and be happy. Would she become a lady, who lived in the white man's world, or choose to live on the ranch or with her tribe?

Laura laughed aloud. Raven would blaze her own trail as Laura had done. They were so much alike—not in looks, but in spirit and nature. These thoughts saddened Laura because she would not be here to see it or be a part of her children's lives much longer.

She placed the final leather journal on the bottom of the others, tying all together with a fringed red ribbon from her past. She glanced around the room making sure everything was the way she wanted to leave it. Her bear claw necklace was in her jewelry box on the table, along with a note bequeathing it to Raven.

She walked slowly down the steps of the cellar to the small safe she had installed years ago. Placing her journals in it for safekeeping, she closed the door, then spun the combination lock. Retracing her steps, she closed the cellar door and thought, *it is as if my life is being closed and sealed.*

The pain overcame her again, and she gripped the back of a chair. It had begun to intensify lately as if a monster ate at her insides. Blood began to flow several days ago, but she said nothing to anyone. When it had passed, she went to her bed to lie down. Stretching out on the quilt her mother had made her long ago, she knew her life was at its end. She had wanted her children near, but now there was no time. She had not known it would happen so quickly.

Nevertheless, she was now at peace. She prayed her children would not grieve too long and would come to know her from her journals and understand the reasons she did the things she did to protect them.

She prayed Talon would come soon to take her and lead her off with him. She missed him so much. Another more powerful ripping agony seized her, and then... she felt a release from the hurt. A wave of darkness began passing over her vision.

Then, there was a bright light and Talon came toward her, dressed in the white buckskins he had worn on their wedding day. Reaching out to her, he beamed, taking her hand in his as he lifted her up saying, "My Spirit Woman, I have loved you from the moment I first saw you coming out of the water. I have missed you so. It is time. Come with me now."

"I've longed for the moment we would be together again, my love," she whispered softly to her Indian lover as he led her into the whirling mists, and into their new journey together.

Silver trailed silently behind them.

THE END

ABOUT THE AUTHOR

*A*ugusta brings her historical fiction to life from past experiences driven by spiritual elements. Her characters come from all walks of life, even the stars. Augusta enjoys light humor in her stories. What could be more relaxing than reading romance with humor? She enjoys writing about strong women who are kind and able to find happiness with an unexpected love.

Augusta lives in the beautiful Texas Hill Country with her family, rescued cats and dogs, and assorted wildlife that wander through. She loves all of God's creatures, except snakes and spiders. She hopes you find pleasure in her books as much as she enjoys writing them.

Embrace the Journey,
Augusta Wright